"Is the baby mine?" Wes demanded.

Justine sucked in a sharp breath. Lying wasn't her style, but she wasn't sure she could tell him the truth. She forced herself to breathe normally, to look him in the eye when she answered. "Why would you even think such a thing?"

"I did the math."

Her gaze slid from his. "Well, yes, I see your point, but you aren't the only man in the world."

"So you were sleeping with someone else when you spent the night with me?" he asked, steel in his voice. "Do you love him?"

"The man who fathered my baby? Yes, I do."

But Justine had taken about all she could. Her nerves were stretched to the breaking point, and she wasn't sure how long she could hold back tears. She turned away from Wes. "What do you want from me?"

She heard him take two steps to reach her. Felt the heat of his body.

You, he wanted to say. "Answers, Justine," he breathed. "I want answers."

Dear Reader,

Though each Special Edition novel is sprinkled with magic, you should know that the authors of your favorite romances are *not* magicians—they're women just like you.

"Romance is a refuge for me. It lifts my spirits." Sound familiar? That's Christine Rimmer's answer to why she reads—and writes—romance. Christine is the author of this month's *The Tycoon's Instant Daughter,* which launches our newest in-line continuity the STOCKWELLS OF TEXAS. Like you, she started out as a reader while she had a multifaceted career—actress, janitor, waitress, phone sales representative. "But I really wanted one job where I wouldn't have to work any other jobs," Christine recalls. Now, thirteen years and thirty-seven books later, Ms. Rimmer is an established voice in Special Edition.

Some other wonderful voices appear this month. Susan Mallery delivers *Unexpectedly Expecting!,* the latest in her LONE STAR CANYON series. Penny Richards's juicy series RUMOR HAS IT... continues with *Judging Justine.* It's love Italian-style with Tracy Sinclair's *Pretend Engagement,* an alluring romance set in Venice. The cat is out of the bag, so to speak, in Diana Whitney's *The Not-So-Secret Baby.* And young Trent Brody is hoping to see his *Beloved Bachelor Dad* happily married in Crystal Green's debut novel.

We aim to give you six novels every month that lift *your* spirits. Tell me what you like about Special Edition. What would you like to see more of in the line? Write to: Silhouette Books, 300 East 42nd St., 6th Floor, New York, NY 10017. I encourage you to be part of making your favorite line even better!

Best,

Karen Taylor Richman
Senior Editor

Please address questions and book requests to:
Silhouette Reader Service
U.S.: 3010 Walden Ave., P.O. Box 1325, Buffalo, NY 14269
Canadian: P.O. Box 609, Fort Erie, Ont. L2A 5X3

Judging Justine

PENNY RICHARDS

Silhouette

SPECIAL EDITION™

Published by Silhouette Books

America's Publisher of Contemporary Romance

This book is for Sandy Steen, fellow laborer,
pseudo-shrink, voice at the end of DIAL-A-PRAYER
and answerer of the panic button.
Thanks for helping keep me relatively sane.

 SILHOUETTE BOOKS

ISBN 0-373-24371-5

JUDGING JUSTINE

Copyright © 2001 by Penny Richards

This edition published by arrangement with Harlequin Books S.A.

® and TM are trademarks of Harlequin Books S.A., used under license.
Trademarks indicated with ® are registered in the United States Patent
and Trademark Office, the Canadian Trade Marks Office and in other
countries.

Visit Silhouette at www.eHarlequin.com

Printed in U.S.A.

Books by Penny Richards

Silhouette Special Edition

The Greatest Gift of All #921
Where Dreams Have Been #949
Sisters #1015
*The Ranger and the
    Schoolmarm* #1136
Wildcatter's Kid #1155
Their Child #1213
The No-Nonsense Nanny #1279
†*Sophie's Scandal* #1359
†*Lara's Lover* #1366
†*Judging Justine* #1371

*Switched at Birth
†Rumor Has It…

Previously published under the
pseudonym Bay Matthews

Silhouette Special Edition

Bittersweet Sacrifice #298
Roses and Regrets #347
Some Warm Hunger #391
Lessons in Loving #420
Amarillo by Morning #464
Summer's Promise #505
Laughter on the Wind #613
Sweet Lies, Satin Sighs #648
Worth Waiting For #825
Hardhearted #859

Silhouette Books

Silhouette Christmas Stories 1989
"A Christmas Carole"

PENNY RICHARDS

has also written under the pseudonym Bay Matthews and has been writing for Silhouette for sixteen years. She's been a cosmetologist, an award-winning artist, and worked briefly as an interior decorator. She also served a brief stint as a short-order cook in her daughter-in-law's café. Claiming *everything* interests her, she collects dolls, books and antiques, and loves movies, reading, cooking, catalogs, redoing old houses, learning how to do anything new, Jeff Bridges, music by Yanni, poetry by Rod McKuen, yard sales and flea markets (she loves finding a bargain), gardening (she's a master gardener) and baseball. She has three children and nine grandchildren and lives in Arkansas with her husband of thirty-six years in a soon-to-be-one-hundred-year-old Queen Anne house listed on the National Register of Historic Places. She supports and works with her local garden club, arts league, literacy council and Friends of the Library. Always behind, she dreams of simplifying her life. Unfortunately, another deadline looms and there is paper to be hung and baseboards to refinish....

All underlined places are fictitious.

Prologue

"Stop right there."

The imperious command was delivered in a gravel-rough voice that dared anyone to disregard it. Wes Grayson, who was wandering through the maze of electrical paraphernalia that littered the backstage area of the auditorium where Justine Sutton had just sung to a sold-out audience, stopped and turned toward the man coming toward him. The guy, wearing black jeans and sweatshirt, was probably approaching sixty but had the body of a much younger man. He looked as if he could have taken on Mike Tyson with no difficulty.

Security, Wes thought.

"I'm not looking for any trouble," he said. "I just wanted to say hello to Ms. Sutton."

"Sorry. Ms. Sutton doesn't accept visitors in her dressing room," the man said, his sharp, watchful gaze giving Wes the once-over.

"We grew up together," Wes said, unwilling to tell this stranger anything more about his relationship with Justine.

"And you are?"

Wes was afraid if he gave his name, Justine would refuse to see him. And now that he'd swallowed his pride and come this far, seeing her seemed mandatory. "Just tell her someone from Lewiston was in town and wants to say hello."

The security guard gave a disdainful roll of his eyes but turned and made his way down the short hallway leading to the dressing rooms. He knocked, was summoned inside and returned a couple of minutes later.

"She said you could come in, but I gotta frisk you."

Wes stiffened.

"Hey," the bodyguard said. "There are a lot of crazies out there, and my job is to keep them far away from her."

Wes thought about that for a couple of seconds. "Sure," he said finally, thinking that if he was willing to be patted down just to see a woman, he wanted to see her pretty badly. Justine had come a long way, too, if she could afford to have a bodyguard. Wes suffered the indignity of the search in silence.

"Okay," the older man said. "Go on in. I'll be right outside."

"Fine," Wes said with a cool nod.

He went down the hall and knocked on the door. It swung open almost immediately. Though he'd played this moment hundreds of times in his mind during the past seventeen years, there was no way he could have prepared himself for the impact of seeing her again. Her lush auburn hair trailed over her shoulders and down her back like a swath of fiery-hued satin. A richly colored Japanese silk kimono was tied at her narrow waist and clung to the ripe curves of her body. She wasn't wearing any makeup—or a bra, one part of his mind noted—and the light sprinkling of copper-colored freckles she hated danced across the creamy smoothness of her nose and cheeks. She didn't need makeup to be the most beautiful woman he'd ever seen. Besides, he'd always loved the freckles.

She was shocked by the sight of him, too. Her mouth was parted in surprise that was mirrored in her green eyes. As he stood there absorbing the sight of her the way someone left stranded in the desert would drink a cupful of liquid, one of her hands came up to clutch the lapels of her robe together. The simple, self-conscious act—voluntary or not—said without words how much things had changed between them. It also brought his borderline lustful thoughts up short.

"Hello, Justine."

She blinked, as if the sound of his voice had brought her back from some faraway place. "What are you doing here?"

Her voice was as he remembered it, only richer, somehow. More full-bodied, like a fine red wine. And like a wine, he sensed that the sound could become intoxicating under the right circumstances.

But not now. Now she was all business. There was no small talk. No chitchat. Just the blunt question that Wes had been asking himself ever since he paid the scalper outside the auditorium a hefty price for a ticket. "I'm in town to talk to Louis Culligan, the owner of the Culligan Art Gallery, about my paintings," he told her.

"So you aren't a lawyer anymore."

"How do you know I ever was?" he queried.

Her smile held a trace of irony. "Just because I left Lewiston doesn't mean I don't keep in touch."

Touch. He wanted to touch her, he realized suddenly. Wanted to thread his fingers through her long red hair and pull her close. Wanted to feel the firm softness of those curves against him, wanted to experience her naked flesh next to him once more and see if her lips were as soft as he remembered.

Hated himself for wanting it.

When he didn't say anything, she asked. "So how did it go?"

"What?" he asked, the unexpected turn of his thoughts making him lose track of the conversation.

"The interview at the gallery."

Wes shoved his hands into the pockets of his jacket. "Louis likes my stuff and wants to do a one-man show when I get enough pieces ready." Wes tried to smile. "Look is it okay if I come in? I feel a little awkward carrying on a conversation in an open doorway."

"I'm sorry," she said, standing aside. "Sure. Come in. I just…I guess I never expected to find you standing in my doorway. You caught me by surprise."

He stepped through the door, and she closed it behind him, shutting him up with her and the memories. She turned and went to the dressing table, putting the width of the small room between them, but her eyes never left his in the mirror. She turned and rested her backside against the built-in vanity, placing her palms on its top. The simple gesture parted the lapels of the robe a bit more, revealing a tantalizing glimpse of cleavage and stretching the thin fabric across her full breasts in a way that sent Wes's heart rate up a notch or two.

"So," she said, once again bringing his erotic

thoughts up short, "if this one-man show is a success, you'll give up lawyering?"

"No. Not anytime soon." He chose his words with care, hoping to elicit some sort of response from her. "Reed and I are partners. I have an obligation to him and the firm. We made some promises when we got out of law school, and I like to think I'm a man of my word."

A flicker of discomfort crossed her face, just as he'd hoped. For almost seventeen years he'd wondered whether or not the things she'd said to him meant anything, or if they were spoken in the throes of the youthful passion that had blazed so hotly between them. Now he knew. She'd meant them. At least at the time.

"Would you like to sit down?" she asked, gesturing toward the white-on-white sofa across the small room. "I was thinking of having Lyle send out for some pizza. I'd be glad to have you join me."

Wes shook his head. "No, thanks. I have a better idea." He ignored the slight, questioning lift of her eyebrows. "I bought this bottle of champagne to celebrate my victory with Louis, but celebration alone isn't much fun. Why don't you come back to my hotel room and we'll toast my success—and yours." He smiled at her and gave a little shrug. "I might even spring for a late dinner."

While her searching gaze probed his, Wes asked himself what he was doing. He'd spent the better half of two decades hating the woman standing in front of him for making him love her, then abandoning him and the feelings he'd believed they shared without a warning or a goodbye. What—besides more pain—did he hope to gain by spending time with her?

He was bracing himself for her refusal when she said,

"That sounds…lovely. You'll have to give me time to get dressed and put on some makeup."

"Put on some jeans," he said. "And forget the makeup. You look fine." *Better than fine.*

"Okay, then. If you'll wait outside, I won't be but a few minutes."

"Sure."

Wes left the room, and Justine stuck her head out the door, called out introductions between the bodyguard and Wes, then disappeared. Wes chatted with Lyle Kennedy while she dressed, knowing the other man was curious about him and wondering if he would stand outside the hotel room door while they shared a meal.

When Justine came out moments later, she was dressed just like Wes. Her hair was tucked up under a black baseball cap, and she wore a pair of black sunshades.

"My disguise," she said, a wry smile lifting the corners of her naked but glistening lips. "With any luck at all maybe everyone will think I'm just a biker chick."

Wes gave a slow shake of his head. "Doubtful." Actually, she looked like what she was: someone trying to disguise who they were.

"Take the night off, Lyle," she said, pressing a bill into his hands. Wes will see to it I get home safely."

Lyle Kennedy's shocked gaze raked Wes from head to toe, clearly finding him wanting as a protector. "Are you sure?"

"Believe it or not, I was boxing champion my senior year of college," Wes said.

Lyle looked doubtful but shrugged massive shoulders. "Okay, boss. Whatever you say."

She gave him a fond smile. "See you in the morning."

They took a cab to the Doubletree, and Wes ordered dinner while Justine wandered around the suite. They drank some of the champagne while they waited for the food, toasting his newest accomplishment and Justine's success and talking about the people of Lewiston.

They had a bottle of wine with their dinner and finished off most of the champagne with their strawberries Romanoff, Wes saying it would be a shame to waste it and they should drink it before it went flat. He wasn't sure if the buzz he felt came from the wine or the intoxicating presence of the woman sitting across from him.

When the CD changer switched to "Memories of Memphis," Justine's most recent, she looked up, surprised.

"I always bring along a few of my favorite CDs wherever I go," Wes said, letting her make of that what she would. "Makes it seem more like home."

"Well, I'm grateful for the success of the CD and for the royalty I'll get from your purchase of it," she added with a cheeky smile. "But I'd rather not listen to it, if you don't mind."

He shrugged, and Justine got up and went to the CD player to study the music selection. "You have very eclectic taste," she said, turning to look at him. "Everything from opera to oldies, flamenco guitar to Enya."

"I'm an eclectic, complex kind of guy," he said, and she smiled slightly before turning away again.

Soon the haunting sound of Kenny G's "Songbird" filled the room. As Justine passed by Wes, who was sitting on the floor near the coffee table, he reached up and grabbed her hand. She looked down at him, the expression on her face part question, part expectation.

He answered the look by giving a sharp tug that elicited a little cry and sent her tumbling onto his lap. Without waiting for her to respond, afraid she'd pull away, he did what he'd wanted to do ever since she'd opened the dressing-room door—what he'd longed to do for years. He kissed her. She struggled to free herself, but Wes wrapped his arms more tightly around her and deepened the kiss.

After the first couple of seconds all the fight went out of her and she kissed him back, trading kiss for drugging kiss. Her lips were as soft as he remembered. But instead of Juicy Fruit, she tasted of strawberries and champagne. Instead of drugstore cologne, she smelled of something clean, fresh and expensive.

Without his being more than marginally aware of what he was doing, he slipped his hand beneath her sweater…and encountered bare flesh. She gave a little cry of surprise but made no move to stop him. At that moment he knew he was lost, knew that his life since she'd left him had been a half-life. Knew he would never be whole again without her.

As they tugged off each other's sweaters and peeled off jeans, he asked himself how Justine Sutton, a nobody from Lewiston, had managed to get so close to him. And why? When she pushed him onto his back, lowered herself on top of him and took his mouth in a hungry kiss, he stopped thinking.

When he woke the next morning, his head pounded with the predictable wine hangover. He raised himself to his elbows and looked around, surprised to see Justine standing near the door, fully dressed.

She drew in a deep breath and smiled a bright, brittle smile. "I had a great time," she said. "Thanks." She shoved on her sunglasses and opened the bedroom door. "Tell everyone back home I said hi."

For the first time in a long time, Wes found himself at a loss for a reply. He wasn't sure how he'd expected her to act, and he certainly wasn't sure what he expected the next step in their relationship to be, but it wasn't this blasé, gee-it-was-fun-I'll-catch-you-later attitude. He was still staring after her and wondering what to make of things when he heard the outer door close with a soft click.

He swung his legs to the floor and sat on the edge of the bed holding his head in his hands and trying to think around the pain that pounded out a monotonous rhythm. Then, realizing he'd done a very foolish thing, he got up, poured himself the dregs of the red wine and drank it thirstily, praying it would take the edge off the pain.

He set the glass on the table and wondered what he'd allowed to happen. How many times had he and Justine made love? Two? Three? He remembered licking the last of the champagne from her body in the big king-size bed and pinning her body to the wall of the shower with his. He checked his wallet. The two condoms he kept there were both gone.

He scrubbed a hand down his face. It was time to get some help. For his drinking and for his seventeen-year obsession with Justine Sutton.

Chapter One

Seven months later

The news that Justine Sutton was back spread through the small town of Lewiston, Arkansas, like a brush fire across a dry prairie on a windy day. With the gas gauge sitting on empty, she was forced to stop to have her bright-red Mustang filled up at the Fina station before going to the hospital where her mother lay dying.

Arnold Grimes didn't recognize her with her fancy car and dark sunglasses, but he recognized her name when she handed him her platinum American Express, and he sure 'nough recognized the fact that she was pregnant when she got out of the car to get a candy bar and Coke from the vending machines.

Even though she'd turned her back on the town and her family when she'd left, she was one of Lewiston's success stories—and a surprising one at that—having made her mark in Nashville, both as a songwriter and more recently as a singer.

As she pulled out onto the street, Arnold's phone rang. It was his wife, asking him to bring home a loaf of bread when he closed up for the day.

"Will do," he said. He was about to hang up when he said proudly, "You'll never guess who just stopped in here to buy gas."

"Who?"

"Justine Sutton. Maybe I can put up a sign out front that says—"

"Justine Sutton?" Mildred interrupted in a scandalized voice. "She must have come back 'cause her mama's dying. How does she look?"

"Like a million bucks, even if she is pregnant."

"I didn't know she was married," Mildred said in a scandalized whisper.

"She's not, to my knowledge." Arnold had stopped being shocked over unwed mothers several years before, when one of the daughters of a local preacher had turned up in the family way. Mildred was different. She and her little coterie of friends thrived on the tidbits of gossip that seemed never ending, even in a town the size of Lewiston, or maybe especially in a town the size of Lewiston. Now, hearing the excitement in his wife's voice, Arnold was sorry he'd mentioned Justine. The news would be all over town in a matter of hours, and Justine Sutton had looked near the end of her rope.

"I hear someone at the door, Arnie," Mildred said. "Gotta go. Don't forget the bread."

There was no one at the door. As Arnold suspected, Mildred hung up and called her two sisters and her two daughters, one of whom had been in the same class as

Justine before she lit out at the age of sixteen. Mildred's daughter took the news to her Saturday-afternoon bowling game, and one of the sisters carried the gossip to her weekly bridge game at Lucille Blair's.

Isabelle Duncan, Lewiston's reigning matriarch and largest stockholder at the bank—who had been dealt a wonderful hand—noted the news with passing interest and said, "Stop gossiping and play cards."

The Lewiston grapevine was hard at work.

Recognition, surreptitious glances and whispers followed Justine as she stopped at the information desk and then made her way down the corridor to the elevator. As clichéd as it was, Justine felt like a bug under a microscope. Because of the business she was in, hers was a familiar face, easily recognizable. She knew her return would be grist for the gossip mill, which was one reason she'd waited so long to come back. Memories, not any of them good, were the other reason.

She pushed the button for the second floor and slumped against the elevator wall, rubbing her distended belly with both hands. The child that seemed to be turning cartwheels inside her was another reason she'd put off her homecoming. Even though having babies out of wedlock was not big news in most places or for most people, Lewiston wasn't most places, and she was Justine Sutton. She hadn't wanted to flaunt her unplanned pregnancy, because she knew it was exactly what everyone expected of her.

She should have come sooner. Her cousin, Sophie, had been after her for months, but Justine had resisted her pleas, uncertain that she could deal with returning to the place and the memories that had left her with deep and ugly scars. But when she received news that her mother was literally at death's door, Justine knew she'd put off the inevitable as long as possible. She'd jumped in her car—she hated flying—and driven from Nashville straight to Lewiston, risking running out of gas. No doubt news of her return and her pregnancy would be all over town in hours, which meant it was only a matter of time before Wes heard. The one slim hope she clung to was that he might not put two and two together. Unfortunately, Wes was a very smart man.

The elevator pinged to a stop, and the doors slid open. Justine pushed herself away from the wall and headed toward the man regarding her with an intent and judging expression in his eyes. Rowland Hardisty. Wealthy, attractive surgeon extraordinaire. Jerk deluxe. Though any interaction with him had been minimal through the years, she'd never liked the man and hoped her sunglasses hid the contempt in her eyes.

"It's about time," he said with his customary lack of tact. "You almost waited too long."

Rowland Hardisty was exactly as Justine remembered him; long on haughtiness, short on bedside manner. Short on manners at all, for that matter; though, as a member of Lewiston's aristocracy, she doubted if he realized it.

"How is she?" she asked.

"Dying."

A sharp shaft of pain she didn't expect pierced Justine's heart, even though she was aware of her mother's deteriorating condition. The pain in her head seemed to intensify. Her aching back seemed about to break in two, and the baby seemed to be doing jumping jacks inside her. She was exhausted, certainly not up for a sparring match.

"Where's her room?" she asked, ignoring his shortness.

Rowland jerked his head to the left. "Third door on the right."

"Thank you."

Aware that his penetrating gaze followed her as she went down the hall, Justine kept her back and shoulders straight. Reaching the third door, she pushed it open on well-oiled hinges. Her cousins, Sophie and Donovan, stood on either side of the narrow bed, each holding a hand of the woman who lay beneath the white thermal blanket. Expecting to find her mother attached to various machines, Justine was surprised by their absence. The only machine in the room was the monitor that tracked the feeble beating of her mother's heart.

As if she sensed someone at the door, Sophie looked up. Recognition lit her eyes, and Donovan turned, smiled and held out his arms. A sweet and consuming joy filled Justine along with equal amounts of regret and sorrow. Why hadn't she made more effort to stay close to her family? She'd learned a lot about fair-weather friends the past few months, and about users. In the final analysis, blood really was thicker than water, and family was all you could count on. Even though she'd rebuffed Sophie's every attempt to draw closer, her cousin had still been there whenever Justine needed to unburden herself. And even though she'd refused Sophie's pleas to come home and make peace with her mother, Sophie had never tried to lay any guilt at Justine's feet.

With a little smile Justine hurried toward Donovan, never more grateful that her cousins weren't the kind to point fingers. As she had, Sophie and Donovan had had enough of that done to them to know how it felt to be on the other side.

Donovan's embrace was strong and warm. Justine thought how nice it would be to have a man to cuddle up to at the end of the day, someone to share the ups and downs of her world—not to mention the nighttime feedings and diaper changes that would soon be part of her life.

When Donovan released her, Sophie gave her a hug and whispered, "I'm so glad you're here. She's been out of her head and asking for you for days, but she stopped mumbling early this morning and hasn't said a word since."

Justine felt an unexpected pang of guilt, though she knew Sophie's brief status report was not designed for that purpose. She gave her cousin another squeeze and moved toward the bed on leaden feet. She wouldn't have recognized her mother if she hadn't known it was she who occupied the bed. Opal was nothing more than skin over bones, her once-wiry body ravaged by the cancer.

Justine felt she should say something. But what? She knew she should reach out and touch her mother, take her hand the way Sophie and Donovan had done, but she couldn't bring herself to do anything more than cling to the bed rails with a white-knuckled grip. She'd come. It was all she could manage.

Sophie went to the other side of the bed and took up her earlier position. Stroking Opal's hand, she said, "Aunt Opal, Justine is here. She's come to see you. Can you hear me? Justine's come home."

Home. How long had it been since she'd thought of Lewiston as home? Suddenly and without warning, a thousand memories rushed Justine, battering at the wall she'd built around her heart. Her mother fixing her hair for the first day of school. The day her mother had taught her how to bake bread. The patience in her voice as she'd explained about planting a garden and the usefulness of various herbs. Sitting on the porch peeling peaches or shelling purple hull peas by the bushel. And then, from the deepest, darkest recess of her memory the one recollection she'd suppressed for seventeen long years came surging out in all its twisted ugliness.

It hit Justine with such force she gave a little cry and actually took a step backward. Thinking her reaction was one of grief, Donovan's arm went around her shoulders, but she tore free of him and stumbled into the hall, fighting without success to stop the sobs that rose up her throat on a dark tide.

Donovan followed her, and this time she let him hold her because she didn't think her legs would keep her upright. Over the sounds of her crying came the chilling statement over the speakers, announcing a code blue. Nurses swarmed Opal's room, Sophie was ejected, and Rowland Hardisty appeared from somewhere beyond the nurse's station.

Filled with dissenting emotions—love, resentment, sorrow and guilt—Justine went a little crazy, trying to pull free and get back into the room. But Donovan held her close, doing his best to comfort her while Sophie looked on helplessly. Within minutes Rowland Hardisty stepped through the doors. His gaze moved from one to the other, coming to rest on Justine, not filled with remorse, but full of judgment and condemnation.

"She's gone," he said, and without a word of condolence or regret, he left her standing there, drowning in her grief and guilt.

Wes was working on some changes to a will when his sister called and asked him if he'd like to have dinner with them.

"I put on a huge roast with carrots and potatoes when I came in at lunch," Lara, who was the high school principal, told him. "Sophie, Reed and Cassidy will be here, but there will be enough for an army."

"You know I never turn down a home-cooked meal," Wes said. "Sounds good." He glanced up and saw Reed standing in the doorway, a frown puckering his brow. "Hey, look, Sis. Something's come up. I gotta go."

"See you later, then."

Wes hung up and looked at his partner. "Well?"

"Arnold Grimes just called and told me he was finished checking out my car," Reed said.

"You need me to take you to pick it up?"

"Yeah, later. Thanks." Reed plunged his hands into the pockets of his suit pants.

"Spit it out, buddy," Wes said. "You look like you just swallowed a green persimmon."

"Arnold also told me Justine is in town. He was all excited that she bought gas from him."

Wes felt the blood drain from his face. No wonder Reed looked so concerned. Reed had been his best friend through the years, as well as his partner and his former brother-in-law. Reed and his new wife, Sophie, and Lara—who'd just recently found out—were the only people in town besides Wes himself who knew he'd dated Justine Sutton back when she was in high school. Reed was the only person who knew that when she left without saying goodbye Wes had gone a little crazy.

"You okay?" Reed asked now, concern in his eyes.

Wes dragged in a deep breath and wiped a hand down

his whisker-stubbled face. "Yeah. I'm fine. Why wouldn't I be?"

"I know how badly she hurt you, and I thought you'd want to know, but I didn't think it would be this big a deal. It was a long time ago."

Wes was too upset to monitor his reply. "Yeah? Well, it wasn't all that long ago, and time didn't change how you and Sophie felt for each other, did it? Or Donovan and Lara? Why should I be different? Because I'm the original poster boy for lovin' and leavin', or because I'm such a cold unfeeling bastard?"

"Whoa!" Reed said, holding out his hands as if to ward off any more verbal abuse. "I'm only the messenger." He crossed the room and took a chair across the desk from Wes. "Let me see if I understand you on this. First, you're upset by the fact that Justine has come back. Any fool can see that."

"I didn't expect it, that's all," Wes grumbled, cocking his chair back and swinging his feet to the top of the antique desk.

"Neither did Sophie," Reed noted. "Okay. I know you saw Justine several times after that first time, but I never thought it was anything serious on your part, but if I heard you right just now, you implied you still feel something for her." The last was posed more as a question than a statement.

Wes made no answer.

"All right. You don't want to say. But exactly what did you mean by it wasn't all that long ago? Seventeen years is quite a spell."

"I saw her in February," Wes said, though he looked pained by the admission. "In Chicago."

Reed whistled. "So that's what happened. We all knew you'd been as touchy as a porcupine with poison ivy, but I, for one, never expected the reason was Justine Sutton. What happened? I take it you actually spent some time with her.''

"About nine hours.''

"Nine—'' Reed began, then broke off when the truth hit him. "You spent the night together?''

Wes swung his feet down and leaped up from the chair, pivoting toward the window that looked out over the tree-lined street. He turned and looked over his shoulder at Reed. "I didn't say that.''

"You don't have to.'' Reed pinned Wes with his most intimidating stare, but his tone was flippant. "Tell me in your own words what happened on that night in February in Chicago, Mr. Grayson.''

Wes turned from the window. "You want all the details?'' he asked angrily. "Fine. I went to see Culligan at the gallery about my paintings. He was interested. I was thrilled. I bought a bottle of champagne and took it to my room. I turned on the television. I don't know why. I saw that Justine was performing, one night only. I got to thinking about old times, and I went to see her.'' The words came in a rush, almost as if he were afraid if he stopped he wouldn't be able to continue.

"She sounded fantastic and looked even better. It had been a long time since there was a woman in my life. I asked her to come to my room for dinner and she agreed. I guess the memories and my libido got the best of me.''

"Are you telling the court you had consensual sex with the lady in question?'' Reed prodded, knowing his friend, knowing that if he slacked up in any way, Wes would clam up on him again.

Wes's lips curved in a wry smile. "Persuading

women to share my bed has never been a problem, counselor.''

"Touché," Reed said smiling back. "Explain what happened during the time you went backstage until—'' Reed waggled his eyebrows à la Tom Selleck ''—and your libido got the best of you, as you phrased it.''

"Objection!'' Wes snapped. "Relevancy.''

"Overruled. It's plenty relevant.''

Wes rolled his eyes, regretting that he'd ever acknowledged anything, knowing Reed wouldn't stop badgering him until he got all the information he wanted.

"I went backstage, just to say hello. We started talking and the next thing I knew, I was asking her up to my room for a late dinner. We had chateaubriand and I opened the champagne. I'm not sure how it happened, but I kissed her, and the next thing I knew, we were on the bed. I woke up and she was heading out the door. She thanked me for a great time and left. No strings. Very modern. I came home. End of story.''

"Not quite,'' Reed said. "Evidently there's more, or you wouldn't be so upset about her coming to town.''

"Yeah, there's more,'' Wes said heavily. "Not a day has gone by that I don't think about that night. About her. Sex was always good between us, even when we were kids. This was dynamite.'' He locked his hands behind his back and began to pace the room. "I need to be painting, and I try, but I can't concentrate. Every woman I paint has Justine's face.''

"It is the opinion of counsel that there's more than sex involved.''

Wes gave short, derisive laugh. "Like what?'' He he.d up a hand. "Don't say love. Just because you and my sister found life in your old loves doesn't mean that's what's wrong with me. What's between me and Justine is just good sex. Besides, I hate her for what she did to me."

"Love. Hate. Two sides of the same coin. Besides, you don't hate anyone or anything. You've just got a long memory and a quick temper."

"And you're crazy if you think that I feel anything but lust for Justine Sutton."

"Do you have a better explanation for your state of mind?"

"No," Wes growled.

Reed smiled and spread his arms wide. "I rest my case."

While Wes and Reed discussed Wes's feelings for Justine, Donovan and Sophie, who were unable to calm Justine's near-hysterical tears, had taken her to the other general practitioner in town. Tom Kincaid was a forty-something widower with a heart of gold and a way of putting people at ease and things in perspective. Tom checked Justine over, gave her a shot of something to take the edge off her emotions, assuring her it would not harm the baby. Then he wrote a prescription for some tablets if she needed them to help her through the next few days. They left Tom's office feeling he could raise the dead, if necessary.

While Sophie stayed with Justine, Donovan called Lara, his wife of little more than three months, to tell her that Opal had died, that he and Sophie would be there soon and that he was bringing Justine home with him, at least for the night.

"She's pretty torn up," he said. "We had to stop by Doc Kincaid's."

"No problem," Lara said. "I put on a big roast when

I came home for lunch. Tell Sophie that Cassidy and Belle are doing their homework, and I already called Reed to tell him he and Sophie may as well eat here. Since they've only been in their house a week, I know they don't have things settled yet." Lara laughed. "Cassidy said if she had to eat another sandwich, she was running away from home."

"I can relate," Donovan said. "Thanks, babe. We'll see you in a little while." He started to hang up, but Lara's voice stopped him.

"Did she make it in time?"

"Yes and no," Donovan said. "She got there literally minutes before Aunt Opal died but not soon enough to have any final words with her."

"I'm so sorry," Lara said.

"Yeah. Look, here they come. I've gotta go. We'll be there in a few minutes."

"Okay. See you then."

By the time they reached the house Donovan had moved into when he married Lara, the shot had done its work, and Justine was asleep. Donovan scooped her into his arms and carried her inside to the downstairs guest bedroom, while Sophie went to help her new sister-in-law in the kitchen.

When Donovan joined them there a few moments later, Lara was loading some dishes into the dishwasher. He put his arms around her waist from behind and pressed a kiss to the side of her neck. "Smells good. So do you, I might add."

Smiling, Lara tipped her head back for a proper kiss and murmured, "Thanks."

"Did you get Justine settled in?" Sophie asked.

Donovan gave a wry smile. "She didn't even stir when I put her down."

"Took it badly, did she?" Lara said, closing the dishwasher and joining him and Sophie at the table.

"Worse than I expected, since she fought so long and hard against coming back," Donovan said, running a hand through his short, dark hair.

"Guilt does that sometimes," Sophie, whose new family-counseling clinic was an unqualified success, offered. "Whatever it is one person holds against another often becomes insignificant when you come up against the realization of losing that someone forever. I can't say what Justine felt when she saw Aunt Opal lying there, but I imagine guilt was right up there next to the sorrow."

Lara nodded in agreement. "You're probably right. What about funeral arrangements?"

"Aunt Opal did all that before she died. She said she didn't want Molly to have to worry with it."

Molly was the younger of Opal Malone's children, born just before Justine left home for good. The sisters hardly knew each other, since Justine hadn't been back to Lewiston since she left, and the times she'd paid for her mother and sister to visit her in Tennessee had been few and far between.

"Does Molly know?"

"I called her," Sophie said. "She's flying in from Dallas tonight. One of her friends is picking her up at the airport in Little Rock."

Molly, a gifted artist with an eye toward advertising, was attending the Dallas Art Institute on full scholarship. Opal hadn't wanted her schooling interrupted, insisting she not be called until it was all over. Sophie and Donovan had respected her decision.

"Well, since things are under control for the moment, I need to go out to the greenhouses for a little while. I'm getting some things together for a landscaping job."

"Go," Lara said making a sweeping gesture with her hands. "You'll just be in the way of us girls."

Donovan smiled and gave her a kiss and promised he'd be back by five-thirty. Saying she needed to check some things at her office, Sophie left for a couple of hours, too. Despite the inevitability of death, life went on.

Lara was at the sink washing greens for a salad and Sophie was peeling potatoes for mashing when Donovan returned ten minutes earlier than he'd predicted.

"Where are my girls?" he asked.

"Upstairs watching music videos," Sophie volunteered, marveling at how easily her brother had stepped into the role of stepfather to Lara's daughter, Belle. "Cassidy is waiting for Jett to call."

Cassidy was the daughter Sophie had borne without Reed's knowledge sixteen years earlier. Belle was the twelve-year-old child Lara and Reed had produced, hoping her arrival would save their deteriorating marriage. All her birth had done was postpone the inevitable. Lara and Reed had been amicably divorced for more than six years.

When Sophie had come back to Lewiston the previous June to help Donovan move and she and Reed discovered they still had feelings for each other, they had decided to give their love a second chance. They had been married a little over two weeks and had just moved from Donovan's place out in the country to a Queen Anne house down the block which they'd spent the past two-and-a-half months restoring.

"Jett's at the university at Fayetteville, isn't he?" Lara asked.

Sophie nodded. "He's dating around, but he still calls Cassidy regularly."

"How old is he?"

"Nineteen," Sophie said. "Too old for Cassidy, but she fell hard for him, and I've learned from my clients that the worst thing I could do was tell her she couldn't see him."

"That's for sure," Lara said.

"They seem to be thinking more clearly than I did at that age," Sophie said. "It was their decision to date other people while Jett is at school. As Cassidy put it, they both wanted to have a good time without feeling any guilt, and if it was meant to be, it would be—whenever." Sophie smiled. "She said she learned that from all of us."

"She has a point," Donovan said. "But it's hard when you have to wait so long for the happy endings."

Lara stood on tiptoe and brushed her lips across his. "Yeah, but the wait was worth it, wasn't it?"

"You bet," he said, reaching for her as she danced away toward the refrigerator.

"Oh, I forgot to tell you that I asked Wes to join us."

Sophie felt a flicker of uneasiness. It had been a long seventeen years since Justine's date with Lara's brother, but considering he'd asked her out solely because she was considered "easy" might make for an uncomfortable evening for both of them, even if her loss would be uppermost on Justine's mind.

"You know your brother is always welcome," Donovan said.

"He's been really moody lately," Lara observed, setting tomatoes, cucumbers and a bell pepper on the countertop.

"I thought moody was Wes's normal behavior," Donovan said.

"Well it is, but it seems as if he's been worse ever since he went to see that gallery owner back in February."

"He's under a lot of stress to produce now," Donovan said. "There's a big difference in creating for your own pleasure and trying to anticipate what someone else might like or want."

"True," Lara said. "And Reed says Wes is exhausted from working so hard. He insists on taking the nastiest cases that come their way."

Donovan gave a so-there-you-have-it shrug. "He's a great attorney. It would be a loss to the town if he ever gets fed up and packs it in."

"I don't think he'll do that," Lara said. "He'll hang in there just to prove to himself that Dad was wrong about him."

Sophie shook her head. "It's amazing the things we do to ourselves because of that little thing called pride. And it's amazing what we do to our kids without meaning to."

"Oh, Dad meant to. Believe me."

The observation came from the doorway where Wes Grayson, clad in faded jeans and a long-sleeved cotton sweater in ice-blue, stood with his hands gripping the white framework on either side of his head. As usual, he needed a shave, but he must have recently found time for the haircuts he usually forgot. All in all his casual appearance was far removed from what clients expected from their attorneys. But Wes's clientele wasn't made up of most people, and he was definitely not your run-of-the-mill lawyer. If convinced of someone's innocence or their stand on a matter, he'd tackle a pro bono case with the same ferver he would if he charged a client a hundred and fifty dollars an hour.

"Hi!" Lara said.

"Hey, Sis. Everybody," he said, nodding toward Sophie and Donovan.

"Come on in and have a seat," Donovan said. "Where's Reed?"

"He's coming," Wes said, crossing the room with an easy grace. He sat down at the kitchen table, across from Donovan. "I drove him to Grimes's gas station to pick up his car, and he said he needed to stop back by the office to pick up some notes on the Lawrey case."

"Lawrey?" Lara asked. "Isn't that the spousal abuse case?"

"Yes," Wes said.

Donovan's lips tightened. He and Sophie and their mom had been victims of abuse. Though they'd managed to become productive citizens and good parents, the torment they'd suffered at their father's hand had left scars that would never go away. "Good thing I'm not the judge. I'd hire a couple of good ol' boys to string up the sorry outfit from the nearest tree."

"Donovan!" Sophie said.

"Sorry. That's the way I feel."

"If it's any consolation, Rowland testified today for the prosecution and did enough damage to send Carl Lawrey up the river for a long time. Reed says the defense will have to work overtime to try to explain away the documented physical abuse Carl inflicted on his family."

"I'm glad he's going to pay for what he's done," Sophie said, carrying the pan of potatoes to the stove.

"I'm afraid that since he found out what Donovan and I lived with, Reed is too emotionally involved in this one."

"He gets way too emotionally involved with all his cases," Wes countered. "Which is why he's such a darn good lawyer."

"That's the pot calling the kettle black," Lara said. "I'd say the two of you rank in the top attorneys in the state."

"Spoken like a true sister." Wes turned to Sophie. "How's your aunt?"

"She passed away a few hours ago," Sophie said.

Wes swore softly. "I'm sorry."

"Yes. Well, at least she isn't suffering anymore."

Justine heard voices and struggled up from the deep depths of her drug-induced sleep.

"She passed away a few hours ago." Sohpie's voice.

Someone was talking about her mama. Her mama passing away. Justine felt an oppressive sorrow welling up deep inside her.

"...at least she isn't suffering anymore."

No. Her mama wasn't suffering. Not anymore. She was dead. Justine's eyes flew open, or it seemed they did, but when she tried to lift her hand to brush at the tears she felt sliding down her temples and into her hair, she could hardly move the leaden weights that were her arms. She realized she had no idea where she was and decided it didn't matter. She was too emotionally exhausted to care. Sophie and Donovan would have seen to it she was somewhere safe. With that thought in mind, she drifted off again...

In the kitchen all was about ready. Donovan had taken Reed outside to show him what he'd been doing to the area around the pool, Sophie was busy setting the table, Cassidy was on the phone with Jett, and Belle was nowhere to be found.

"Wes, do you mind going to see if Justine feels like getting up to eat?" Lara asked.

Stunned by the request, he said, "Justine?"

Sophie must have been surprised by the request, too, because she shot a startled look at Lara, who was adding thickening to the gravy and didn't appear to realize her entreaty was out of the ordinary.

She spared him a brief glance and returned her concentration on her task. "She's in the bedroom down the hall. She was so upset about her mother that Sophie and Donovan had to take her to see Tom Kincaid. He gave her a sedative, but she might be awake enough to join us."

When he didn't answer, she glanced at him again. "If you can't rouse her, that's fine. She can always eat when she does wake up."

"Sure," Wes said agreeably, pushing back his chair and heading toward the door that led to the hallway. He'd never admit that his heart was pounding ninety to nothing, but it was.

The door to the downstairs guest room was across the hall from the room Lara and Donovan shared. Wes rapped softly on the raised panel, waited, and when there was no answer, he turned the knob and eased the door open. Justine lay on her side, her hair spreading over the comforter like a flame, one hand beneath her cheek. The light throw covering her warmed her against the chill of the air-conditioning that was still necessary even though it was mid-September.

Wes shoved his hands into his pockets and moved

closer to the bed, stifling the urge to reach out and touch her. She looked pale, he thought, noting the honey-colored freckles across her nose and the dark circles beneath her eyes. But maybe it was nothing more than the fact that her makeup had worn away throughout the day and her mascara had run from her crying.

She looked weary and fragile and no doubt was. Time had soothed the pain of his mother's death, but he did remember that both he and Lara had cried for days because they missed her and didn't understand the permanence of her leaving. He could only compare what Justine must be going through to the way he'd felt when she'd left town so many years before. Sad. Empty. Helpless. The anger had come later, and it had been years before he'd gotten over it, finally chalking up her flight from Lewiston to a need she must have had to get away, something he understood on some level.

He was surprised that he'd felt no anger after their one-night stand in Chicago, only the aching emptiness that came with knowing he'd have to come back to Lewiston to his lonely existence, where there was nothing but work and painting and the occasional woman to ease the desire he couldn't always squelch. Chicago had made him admit what some part of him had always known and wouldn't acknowledge: he loved her. He had loved her when she was sixteen and wore cheap flashy clothes, and he loved her now that she was a success who'd traded in cheap for chic. No other woman made him feel the way she did. No other woman felt like Justine in his arms. No other woman made him feel whole, complete.

Despite his determination not to, he took his hand from his pocket and brushed the knuckle of his index finger across the curve of her cheekbone. The urge to bend over and kiss her was almost overwhelming. She murmured something unintelligible and stirred, rolling to her back and flinging one arm over her head.

Wes stared at her in disbelief. Beneath the throw, her belly was a hard, round mound. Wes's gut clenched, and he felt as if his legs might give way. Justine was pregnant!

The fragile dreams that had been his sustenance crumbled along with whatever frail hope he might have had of them somehow getting together…something he'd toyed with on days loneliness and despair ate into his soul like a canker.

Whose child was it? And how far along could she be? Afraid to think about that, not really wanting to know the answer, he backed toward the open door and closed it behind him with a soft click.

Chapter Two

Justine drifted in and out of sleep, the knowledge of her mother's death following her wherever she went. Asleep, she dreamed of good times. Approaching wakefulness, she felt the stinging pain of her loss, felt the full weight of the guilt begin to sink its talons deep into her soul. Justine was always one to be swayed by guilt. She excelled at guilt. Unable to cope with the pain or the guilt, she let the comforting sea of the sedative drag her back under.

She felt something as light as butterfly's kiss brush at her cheek. Real or imagined, it nudged her toward wakefulness. Murmuring, she rolled over and lifted an arm over her eyes. The baby stirred, letting her know he was awake, too. She moved her hands to her abdomen and felt him kick strongly. He. Somehow she sensed Wes's child was a boy, even though she hadn't wanted to be told the baby's sex when she'd had the ultrasound.

What would Wes say if he knew he was going to be a father? That she was going to be the mother of his baby? Did he even want children, or did he consider children, like a wife, an encumbrance? Men like Wes—brilliant, handsome, wealthy—seemed above such mundane things as taking out the trash or sitting up with a colicky baby.

As she grew more awake, her worry mutated into self-directed anger. How had it happened? Why had she let it happen? She had been cleaning the stage makeup from her face when a knock had sounded at her dressing-room door.

"Yes?" she'd called, reaching for a jar of moisturizer.

"It's me."

"Come on in, Lyle."

Lyle Kennedy, the aging ex-boxer who acted as her bodyguard, had slipped into the room. Their eyes had met in the mirror. "You've got a visitor."

"Who is it?"

"He won't give his name but says he's from your hometown."

She frowned. "Lewiston?"

"That's what the man said."

Intrigued, she turned and asked, "What does he look like? Old? Young? What?"

"Late thirties. Dark hair. Tall. Well dressed," Lyle said with a shrug.

Justine racked her mind for someone from Lewiston who would actually look her up if they happened to be in Chicago. She drew a blank.

"He doesn't look like a killer or a rapist, does he?" she asked with a smile.

"No," Lyle said. "But there is something dangerous about him."

She raised her eyebrows. "Dangerous, huh? Sounds interesting. What the heck," she said. "Frisk him and send him in. And stay close, okay?"

"You bet."

Lyle left. In a matter of minutes there was another sharp rapping at the door. Justine swung it open, a soft smile of welcome on her lips. When she recognized the man standing there, the smile faded like a moonflower at dawn.

Wes.

She hadn't seen him since she'd left Lewiston, but she did take the weekly paper, and his picture occasionally graced the pages. Wearing black jeans, a black crew neck sweater and a black leather jacket, he looked much younger than his thirty-six years. His hair—as black as his eyes and needing a cutting—and the day's growth of beard on his lean cheeks gave him a tough, sexy look. Sin incarnate. Every woman's most dangerous fantasy. And she knew for a fact that he was that— dangerous.

She also knew that nothing had changed in the years they'd been apart. She'd had other relationships since leaving Lewiston, and she'd convinced herself that at least two of them were the real thing. Funny how you forgot exactly what the real thing was until it was staring you in the face. The real thing was Wes Grayson.

Shock—at seeing him and at realizing that the feelings she'd once had for him were thriving, not dead as she'd imagined—robbed her of speech. He didn't say anything, either. She had no idea how long they stood there, neither speaking, just staring at each other. She wondered if he was remembering the times they'd spent together at his father's cabin on Crescent Lake, making out under a mountain of blankets so heavy they could hardly move. Of making love in the big clawfoot tub. On a blanket under the spreading arms of the mimosa tree. On the dock. In front of the fire.

And the talking. Did he ever think about how they'd shared their dreams, their hopes, their fears? Did he remember that she worried about her mama and that her dream had been to be the best mother she could, to never let her children down? Had he forgotten that he'd told her how he would never measure up to his dad's dreams and that he would be a better dad than Phil Grayson ever could be? Did he recall how they'd fed each other popcorn and ice cream, and how they'd played Monopoly and Scrabble and walked in the woods and toasted marshmallows in the fireplace? Did he remember the sweet purity of their passion and how much they'd loved each other? Or did he still hate her for leaving him without a word of explanation?

She couldn't tell. There was nothing in his eyes to give him away. Finally he'd said simply, "Hi."

"Hi," she'd replied, and asked him in.

Though conversation had been strained at first, he'd become more animated as he'd told her about his talk with Louis Culligan at the gallery. Then he'd said he had a bottle of good champagne at his hotel room and asked if she would like to help him celebrate over a late dinner. She'd gone, knowing that accepting was an invitation to heartbreak. The dinner was exquisite. The champagne was divine, the second bottle even better. The lovemaking was glorious.

How *had* it happened? When she'd gone to change

the music on the CD player, he'd grabbed her hand and pulled her onto his lap. Things had gotten out of hand from there. She wasn't sure how many times they'd made love, but she did recall it being the most intense physical encounter she'd ever experienced, the most satisfying emotional experience of her life. With every touch, every kiss, every movement of his lean, hard body, he had plumbed depths and taken her to heights she knew no other man could ever hope to rival. He'd made her moan with delight, cry out with passion and shed tears of complete and total satisfaction. She'd been consoled by the knowledge that his response to her was just as absolute.

It wasn't until she'd awakened the next morning that the full implication of her foolishness hit her. Determined not to place blame—after all, she could have said no—and equally resolute about not being dumped, she'd donned her clothes and her most blasé attitude, thanked him for a perfectly wonderful night and sashayed out of his hotel room and his life…for the second time.

He hadn't called. She hadn't expected him to. It had been a moment out of time, something she blamed on the champagne and loneliness. And here she was, seven months' pregnant with his baby. She drew in a deep, steadying breath and smelled something wonderful wafting on the air. Her stomach growled, grounding her in reality. She was hungry and rightly so. She'd been in such a hurry to get here she hadn't stopped to eat anything but part of the candy bar she'd bought from Arnold Grimes.

She sat up slowly and looked around the room, letting her spinning head catch up with the rest of her body. There was a picture of Donovan and Lara on an antique highboy. Most likely, she was at their house, since Sophie wasn't settled in yet.

Justine got to her feet and crossed the room to the door. The floral runner of the hallway muffled her footsteps as she made her way toward the voices. In the kitchen Lara was stirring something on the stove, and Sophie was rummaging in a drawer. Three men sat at the round oak table: Donovan and Reed—she'd have known him anywhere, even though it had been seventeen years since she'd seen him. The third man was Wes. Shock paralyzed her. What was he doing here?

She must have made some sound, because every eye in the room turned to her. No one was smiling. Instead, Sophie, Donovan, Lara and Reed all looked concerned. Wes's face wore what could only be described as a considering expression. His dark eyes probed hers. Then, as she'd known it would, his gaze traveled over her body then moved back to hers.

The entire episode couldn't have taken more than a second, but it felt like aeons to Justine whose head was spinning in a disbelief of her own. Somehow she'd expected him to be completely surprised when he saw her condition, but he wasn't.

Why should he be, Justine? Everyone in the world knows. Hasn't it been the topic of every television news show and every gossip rag in the country—not to mention being discussed at length on CMT and TNN?

Donovan's voice broke what felt to Justine like total silence. "Hi." He asked in that deep Sam Elliot-like voice, "How're you feeling?"

She forced a smile. "Not bad, considering." Ignoring Wes, she turned to Lara. "Something smells really good, and I'm starving."

"Thanks," Lara said. "Everything's almost ready."

Then, ever the proper hostess, she added, "In case you don't recognize him, this is my brother, Wes. Wes, you remember Sophie and Donovan's cousin, Justine, don't you?"

Justine was forced to look at him.

"We've met," Wes said.

"Yeah," she said. "Briefly. A long time ago." She consoled herself with the knowledge that the statement wasn't exactly a lie. Justine noticed that Reed shot a troubled look from her to Wes. How much did he really know about their past? Then, deftly changing the subject, Reed offered his condolences.

"We need to contact the funeral home and set a time for the service," Sophie said.

"I know." Justine pushed back a swath of heavy auburn hair. "I was thinking Monday morning if Molly gets here tonight. There's no one else coming from out of town, and there's no sense prolonging things."

"I'm sure that would be fine," Sophie said. "We're already getting calls about food."

Food, Justine thought. If things were like they used to be, people would come in droves. They'd come bearing casseroles and fried chicken and home-baked cakes, under the guise of paying their last respects, when what most of them really wanted was to get a look at her. Some would stop by hoping to get a glance at country's newest singing sensation. Others would come to see if the rumors about her pregnancy were true. Still others just wanted to pass judgment on her because she'd left the place of her birth and never came back, not even when her mama got sick. Not until she was all but dead. Justine wasn't sure she wanted to be on display for the citizenry of Lewiston.

"How long can you stay?" Donovan asked, pulling

out a chair for her across the table from Wes. She was aware of Wes's eyes on her, assessing her and finding her wanting.

Not long. Hopefully before I have to spend any real time with Wes.

"I'm not sure. I need to get back as soon as possible." A lie. There was nothing much happening with her career since her manager had left her stranded because of her decision to keep the baby. She was considering another manager and had been looking at new songs for her next CD, but there was nothing pressing. "I want to make sure Molly's okay, and I thought I'd stay and help her go through Mama's things. If she's going to be staying at the house, she won't want a lot of reminders around."

"When's the baby due?"

Considering the topic of discussion, the question came as a surprise, especially since Wes asked it.

She thought about lying but, considering how easily she'd fallen into bed with him, Wes had probably never considered the possibility that the baby was his. He no doubt thought her actions the night they'd spent together were indicative of her way of life. She forced a steadiness she was far from feeling to her gaze, and her voice and opted for the truth. "Mid-November."

Maybe she'd misjudged him. A mistake, she knew. She could almost see the wheels turning inside his head as he did some mental calculating. She knew the precise instant he made the connection to mid-February. It was there in the subtle tensing of his body and the tightening of his lips. In the thoughtful expression that entered his eyes.

Justine shifted in her chair, wondering what he would say to that.

"Good!" Lara said, salvaging the moment. "You'll have it over with before the holidays."

"Yeah. I can trade in my rotund figure and heartburn for midnight feedings," Justine said making a stab at acting normal.

"Is that a fair trade for a woman in your situation? A crying baby for your figure back?" Wes rested one arm on the table and regarded her with a steady expression.

"Wes!" Lara chided. "Where are your manners?"

Justine summoned a smile. There was nothing overtly condemning in his voice, nothing she hadn't been asked before during interviews and by fans. It was just the little something in his eyes that said his interest was more than idle curiosity and made the question a near dig. The only thing that might keep the others from becoming suspicious was that Wes's reputation as a hot-shot attorney had been based on his irreverence and insolence and his willingness to demand answers to the hard questions.

"It's okay," she said, glancing at Lara. "I don't mind answering." She faced him with a steady look. "I'll answer your question if you'll explain what you mean by a 'woman in my situation.'"

He gave a slight shrug. "You're in the limelight. You're a beautiful woman. Your career is taking off. I just wondered how you felt about having a baby just now."

"Well, it certainly wasn't planned," she said. "And I'll admit the timing stinks, but I'm not getting any younger, Mr. Grayson, and—"

"Wes," he interjected, propping his chin on his palm.

Justine felt hot color creep into her cheeks. Oh, he

knew how to play it cool, all right. "Wes, then," she said with a tight smile. "As inconvenient as it is, as deathly sick as I've been, and for all that it has thrown a major kink in my life, I wouldn't trade my career or my former figure for one hair of this baby's head."

Wes didn't reply. From the silence that filled the room, Justine knew that their exchange had given the other occupants plenty to think about.

"The gravy is ready," Lara said, breaking the almost tangible tension. "Let's eat."

The meal went better than Justine expected. Neither she nor Wes contributed much to the conversation, but there were so many people around the dining table she didn't think anyone noticed. She did detect the occasional look of concern on her cousins' faces, and she noted what could only be called expressions of downright worry when she happened to intercept their covert glances. She saw at least one what's-going-on? look pass from Lara to Wes.

Justine worried that somehow everyone knew the truth and reminded herself that that was impossible. She *had* told Sophie she'd gotten pregnant in Chicago, but she hadn't revealed the name of the man responsible. Still, her cousin hadn't become a successful psychologist by letting seemingly unimportant details slip past her.

As soon as Cassidy and Belle—who'd asked for Justine's autograph—cleared the table of everything but the dessert plates, Wes, claiming a horrendous workload, excused himself and bade everyone good-night. Lara and Reed walked him to the door. Justine watched him go with a mixture of relief and sorrow. She was making hieroglyphics with her fork in the chocolate pie filling clinging to her plate when Sophie said, "You're whipped, aren't you?"

Justine glanced at her cousin with a weary smile. "Yeah, I am."

"Are you staying at your mother's place?" Lara, who had just returned to the room, asked.

"No!" Justine's answer was sharp and emphatic. "I…I can't."

"That's understandable," Sophie said. "Why don't you stay with me and Reed?"

"Oh, Sophie!" Lara chimed in. "You're barely unpacked. She can stay with us."

Justine glanced from one woman to the other. She had no doubts that their intentions were good, but she wasn't up to being a houseguest. She just wanted to be alone to grieve and remember and lick her wounds. "I appreciate the offers, but I don't want to inconvenience anyone. I'll just get a room at the hotel."

"Mabel's?" Lara said with a shake of her head. "She's more of a boarding house for the social-security set these days. I don't think you'd be very comfortable there."

"My place is empty since Sophie moved out," Donovan said. "You're welcome to stay there. Molly, too, when she comes."

Donovan's place. Aunt Ruby's house. She knew Donovan had made some major renovations, but the house where she'd spent so much time as a child would still offer the comfort of familiarity without weighing her down with unwanted memories. She offered him a soft smile. "I think I'd like that. Thanks."

"I'll drive you out," he said.

"I can drive myself," she insisted. "I've put everyone out enough."

"Unfortunately, since you were in no condition to drive earlier, Sophie and I left your car in the hospital parking lot. We figured it would be fine there until we could pick it up tomorrow. I did get your suitcases, though."

Justine gave a little inward cringe at the reminder of how she'd lost control at the hospital. She'd caused everyone enough trouble—not to mention that her cousins had probably been embarrassed by her behavior. There was no sense putting them out any more by asking them to let her pick up her car tonight, since she didn't plan on going anywhere.

"That's fine," she said, pushing herself to her feet. "And I hate to be a party pooper, but I'm past ready to call it a day. Whatever that doctor gave me is powerful stuff."

"I'll drive you," Donovan offered again, grinning. "Sophie can stay here and help Lara with the dishes."

Sophie glanced at Justine and said, "Your cousin is a sexist pig." She was smiling when she said it, and Justine knew it was spoken in jest. If anything, there were few men who showed women as much respect as Donovan. Wes, who epitomized the Southern gentleman, was one of them.

"Oink, oink," Donovan replied, completely unrepentant. "Come on, Juss, let's go. If you're nice, I might stop by the Dairy Delight and buy you a chocolate milk shake."

"You just had chocolate pie!" Lara cried in astonishment. Justine flashed Sophie a smile. Clearly Donovan's new wife hadn't grown accustomed to Donovan's legendary sweet tooth. "Where do you put it all?"

"I'm a growing boy," he said.

"You're going to be growing, all right," she said. "Fat."

Donovan put his arms around her and rubbed his nose against hers. "It's your job as my loving wife to see to it that I burn off all those nasty calories."

Lara gave a shake of her head and an exaggerated sigh. "Well, I certainly wouldn't want anyone claiming I didn't do my wifely duty," she said in a resigned voice. "So I suppose I'll just have to grin and bear it."

Donovan released her and stepped back, a hand over his heart. "Grin and bear it? I'm crushed. My ego is smashed to smithereens."

Lara jabbed his hard middle with her elbow and Donovan laughed and turned to Justine. "The woman didn't even know what a sense of humor was a few months ago. Now she can fire off a comeback faster than I can."

"If you can't stand the heat, get out of the kitchen," Justine said.

Donovan threw up his hands. "I can see I'm out-numbered." He held out his hand to Justine. "Come on, cuz, let's go."

Reed, who must have been outside talking to Wes, came back into the room. "Are you leaving?" he asked Justine.

"I'm beat," Justine said with a nod. "It was good to see you again, Reed." She accepted hugs and condolences and well wishes and preceded Donovan out to his sports utility vehicle.

He helped her in, and they took off down the street. A couple of blocks away, he pointed to a gray two-story Queen Anne house sitting in the middle of a huge corner lot with several giant oaks and crape myrtles dotting the yard. "That's Sophie and Reed's new place. They've spent a fortune fixing it up."

"It's gorgeous," Justine said. "Is she happy here, Donovan?"

Donovan glanced over at her. "Happier than she's been since Jake died. As much as she loved him, she never got over Reed. Not completely."

"And you never got over Lara."

"No."

"I didn't even know you dated her."

"That was the plan," Donovan said. "There was a lot of that secret stuff going around that summer, wasn't there?"

Justine stiffened. Did he know about her and Wes then? Or was he trying to see if he could trip her up? "I beg your pardon?"

"Me and Lara. Sophie and Reed. Lots of secret liaisons."

The breath Justine had been holding trickled out in a sigh of relief. She let her head fall back against the headrest and closed her eyes. So he wasn't fishing. Just commenting on the relationships he knew about. "So it seems."

It was less than a ten-minute drive from Donovan's house in town to the place he'd grown up; nevertheless, Justine must have dozed, because the next thing she knew, the Explorer was bouncing down a gravel lane. She sat up. Far beyond the house, four greenhouses sat, their heavy plastic coverings gleaming whitely in the glow of several tall nightlights scattered around.

"Wow! You really are in the landscape business," she said with a laugh. "Is it going okay?"

"It's going great," he said. "Better than I hoped."

"That's good. You deserve it."

"And so do you."

Justine's antennae went up again. "What do you mean? I've got the world by the tail."

Donovan pulled to a stop in front of the house. "Do you?"

Another little twinge of apprehension fluttered through her. "Have you seen the country music charts this week?"

"I'm not talking about your musical success, Juss. I'm talking about your personal life. Sophie and I worry about you."

"Which translates to who the heck is the father of my baby?"

"I don't give a damn who the father of your baby is," Donovan said, the truth of the statement in his tone. "I care that for some reason he isn't around. I care that even though you're giving an outstanding performance of someone who can go it alone, you wish he was. I care because I know that something terrible happened to you before you left and you've never talked about it. I care about the fact that underneath all that bravado you're lonely and scared."

Justine's answer was a laugh so brittle a breath of wind would have shattered it. "I never could hide my feelings from you."

"And you never will be able to," Donovan said. Without waiting for her to answer, he opened the door. "Come on. I'll give you the grand tour and let you get settled in for the night.

"I'm past ready," Justine said.

At the door Donovan unlocked the dead bolt and handed her the key. "Do yourself a favor," he said before opening the door.

"What's that?"

"Talk to Sophie. Get it all off your chest. If you don't get it out, it will fester even more. Sophie won't judge you. None of us will. You know that."

His suggestion was something she'd been thinking about for several months...ever since Wes had made a brief reappearance into her life...ever since her mama got sick. Ever since the memories had started invading her sleep.

"Yeah," she said. "I know. And I've been thinking of talking to her. Really."

"Don't just think about it," Donovan urged. "Do it."

From the relative anonymity of two blocks, Wes followed Donovan's vehicle until it reached the edge of town. Realizing Donovan was taking Justine to his place for the night, Wes turned around and headed toward his house by the lake. His first inclination had been to follow them and, when Donovan left, to confront Justine about whether or not he was the father of her baby. Common sense prevailed.

Back when he drank, his temper had been legendary—as explosive as a Molotov cocktail and as easily inflamed as cherries jubilee. Sober, he was better able to rein in his emotions. He was too upset by the sight of Justine to carry on a rational conversation just now, and besides, she'd just lost her mother. The timing for a showdown was way off.

He swore and hit the steering wheel with his fist. When she'd rolled over in Lara's guest room and he'd seen she was pregnant, he'd been too shocked to feel much more than that. A loner by nature, Wes only went to the grocery store when there was absolutely nothing left in the house to eat. He wore expensive clothes with timeless style, seldom turned on the television and often let the newspapers stack up unread, so even though he had a general idea of what had happened in her life since she left, he had known nothing about the baby until she'd rolled over and he'd seen the undeniable proof of her pregnancy. Justine pregnant with a baby that could very well be his.

What are you going to do about that, Grayson?

What he was going to do was sleep on it and see if he could manage a meeting with her as soon as Opal Malone was buried. He needed to know the truth.

Why? If it is your baby, it's pretty clear she doesn't want anything from you, or she'd have contacted you by now. Still, he needed to know. Wanted to. Wes tried to imagine himself as a father and couldn't form a mental image of him doing anything fatherly. He hadn't exactly had a good example in his own father. He could see Justine with a baby, though. It was easy to imagine her singing a child to sleep, effortless to picture her nursing a baby at her full breasts.

How could she do this to him?

Do what, Grayson? Whoever the father is, it didn't happen by immaculate conception. If it is your baby, you're as much to blame as she is. More, maybe. After all, you're the one who made the first move. You're the one who had the protection.

Placing blame was useless. If anything, the blame was mutual. What had happened, had happened. As Aunt Isabelle would say, there was no use crying over spilt milk. If he was the one responsible for protection, she was the one whose total abandon had inflamed him over and over. She'd always had that effect on him. No, they'd always had that effect on each other. If the moans and groans and ferver of her response was any indication, there was no doubt that Justine had enjoyed their night together as much as he had.

From somewhere deep inside him came a memory he hadn't recalled before—Justine turning away from him. His hand curling around a softness of her shoulder and turning her to face him. Tears flooding her eyes.

When he'd asked her what was wrong, she'd given a shake of her head and reached up to caress his cheek with her fingertips. As he'd gathered her close, he recalled feeling macho and protective and...thankful. They had fallen asleep in each other's arms, and when he'd awakened, Justine was dressed and heading out the door; the moment and the night seemingly forgotten. Remembering, Wes knew now that that was why he'd been so stunned by her behavior as she'd gone...why he'd been so surprised by her going at all.

Why had he forgotten the tearful incident until now? Why, now that he had remembered, did he feel so uncomfortable? And what was it about Justine that he found so captivating, even after so many years? More important, why couldn't he forget her after the way she'd walked out of his life without so much as a goodbye?

At sixteen Justine had had a reputation for being easy, so when Reed, who was taken with Sophie, had suggested a double date, Wes, who'd had a young man's preoccupation with sex, couldn't wait to find out if the rumors were true.

She hadn't been a virgin, but she wasn't experienced, either. Justine had proved a quick study, and it hadn't taken long for him to teach her everything he'd known about the forbidden act. Soon they were meeting at the lake house every chance they could. It was during those times that Justine taught Wes some things, too. Though he made her laugh, there were times she was quiet, moody…maybe more moody than he himself was.

He soon realized that even with her poor upbringing and beneath the flashy clothes she wore there was an inherently good person. She never cursed, could never be talked into drinking anything alcoholic and believed in the biblical premises of good overcoming evil and turning the other cheek. She was smart, making As and Bs at school.

Wes had fallen for her fast and hard. She was the anchor in his life, the steadying force. The sunshine in his world. And then one day she'd said she thought they were getting too serious. She'd left town the next day— without an explanation or a goodbye—and he hadn't seen her again until Chicago.

She'd broken his heart, and as usual, when hit with emotions too painful to deal with, he retaliated in anger, becoming the poster boy for the surly, hard-drinking, hard-loving college boy. Time had eased some of the pain, though he'd never really forgotten her.

There had been other women through the years. Lots of them: rich debutantes whose only desire was to perpetuate the lifestyle of the upper class and the species by marrying well and producing little carbon copies of themselves; smart women; polished professionals with strings of degrees who were stimulated by his intelligence; women in the arts who shared a common interest, who understood both the creative process and his moods.

He'd come close to marrying three of them but had called off the weddings at the last moment, realizing it would be the height of unfairness to enter into marriage without loving them the way they thought he did. The way they deserved to be loved. Because no matter who it was who shared his bed, Justine kept him from sharing his heart.

He swore and flipped on the blinker before turning into the wooded lane that led to his house on the lake. After the funeral on Monday he would make it a point to talk to her before she left town. He'd demand to know the truth. He wasn't sure where he'd go from there.

Chapter Three

Justine awoke on Sunday morning to the chattering of birds outside the window. It took her a couple of seconds to realize where she was—Donovan's place—and when she did, the *why* she was there came rushing back. Her mother was dead, and sometime today she would have to finalize the funeral plans and deal with her younger sister, Molly, a virtual stranger.

And whose fault is that, Justine?

Hers, of course. It wasn't that she and Molly didn't get along; it was that they hardly knew each other, something Justine knew was her fault. Her mother had done everything in her power to stay in touch, to try to maintain their relationship. Opal had preached constantly that one day Justine would regret not forging a relationship with Molly. But doing that would have meant dealing with things Justine would rather not deal with, and when she'd left seventeen years earlier, she'd cut all ties to her life in Lewiston, including those to her mother and sister. She knew no one understood, not even her cousins, who wondered what had happened to cause the estrangement. Justine couldn't bring herself to talk about it, and distancing herself physically and mentally was the only way Justine knew to survive.

And she had survived. The irony was that though she'd turned her back on Lewiston and her past, here she was, back in the thick of things—same people, same situations. She hadn't eliminated the confrontation with Wes so long ago. All she'd done was postpone it.

Wes. Justine's hand moved to her abdomen where his baby was just beginning to stir. His face was the last thing she remembered before she'd fallen asleep the night before. How was she going to deal with him? What could she say? It was her way to keep her silence and evade the truth in a sticky situation as long as possible, but if he demanded to know if he was the father of her baby, she wasn't sure what she would do. Outright lying wasn't something she was comfortable with, but on the other hand, she didn't think she could tell him the truth. Of course there was the off chance that if he found out the truth, he would want the baby and not her. There was no way she could compete with a Grayson in a custody battle. Not only was Wes filthy rich, he was a superb attorney.

Maybe he'd keep his distance. Maybe he wouldn't ask.

Yeah, right. And maybe the past could be undone. Thickness rose in Justine's throat, and hot moisture gathered in her eyes. Like a child, she ground her fists into her eye sockets to blot away the tears. The baby kicked, reminding her that nothing could be undone. Bad things and mistakes could be dealt with, or you could try to ignore them, but they didn't go away, and they could never be changed.

The problem was that she'd been trying to pretend the past hadn't happened. As a teenager, she'd thought that if she put enough space between her and Lewiston, she could forget. She hadn't, so she'd tried working herself into the ground. That hadn't solved the problem, either. Her uncle Hutch's drinking had shown her the pitfalls of alcohol, so that was out, except for the occasional glass of wine. Her only viable option had been to try to stay far away from the place and the people that triggered the bad memories.

Justine gave a groan of frustration and swung her feet to the side of the bed. She couldn't dwell on the past and its problems, especially since she had a new problem. Molly was supposed to arrive late the night before, and they had to finalize the service for their mother.

A rapid knocking sounded at the front door. Surely it wasn't Molly so early. Justine got up and went to the door in her oversize, knee-length nightshirt. To her surprise and relief, she saw Sophie with a wide smile on her face.

"You up?"

"I am now," Justine said in a sleep-roughened voice.

"Kind and considerate cousin that I am, I thought I'd come fix you breakfast. Pamper you a little."

"Sounds good," Justine said, stepping aside. "Come on in. I hope there's food, because I sure didn't bring any."

"There is. You know Donovan. He never likes to stop for anything when he's working, and he's always hungry, so he keeps a few things here."

"This is really sweet of you, Sophie, but won't Reed want his breakfast?" Justine asked, following her cousin into the combination kitchen-dining area and taking a seat at the antique oak table.

"Reed is just thankful I let him sleep instead of waking him to unpack boxes. He worked on the Lawrey case until all hours last night. I doubt if he gets up before noon." Sophie opened the refrigerator and brought out a can of coffee. "First things first. Or do you drink coffee?"

"I have a cup in the morning now that I'm not so sick," Justine said. "Other than that, I try to stay away from it."

"I remember those days well," Sophie said, scooping coffee into a brown paper filter.

"So do you plan to do it again?"

Frowning, Sophie glanced up from her task. "What? Have another baby?"

"Yeah."

"I'm not planning on it." Justine could see the question had flustered her unflappable cousin. "I mean…I have a child by Reed, and I'm not sure I want to go through all that again at my age. But if we slip up—" she shrugged "—I don't think either of us would be too upset."

"So it's working out okay? You got everything resolved?" Justine asked.

Sophie nodded and turned on the coffeepot. "Reed and I realize we never stopped caring for each other and that things might have been different if our fathers hadn't manipulated our lives. We're trying to get to know the people we've become. And he and Cassidy are both working hard on the father-daughter relationship."

"She adored Jake, didn't she?"

"Jake Carlisle was the only father she ever knew,"

Sophie said. "Finding out Reed is her real dad can't have been easy. And then there's Belle."

A look of surprise crossed Justine's face. "I'd forgotten that Reed and Lara have a daughter, which makes you a stepmom. How's that working out?"

"Couldn't be better," Sophie said, holding up crossed fingers. "I know we'll clash somewhere down the line, but right now things are fine. She's a great kid." Sophie shrugged. "How can she not be when Lara and Reed are both such good people?"

"You know this whole divorced-but-still-good-friends thing is a little weird," Justine said.

"I know. But Reed and Lara's situation was a lot different from that of a lot of divorced couples," Sophie said. "And even if they hadn't divorced amicably, I don't understand why it should be unnatural to maintain a civil relationship. I know that there are often terrible reasons for a divorce—abuse, infidelity—but if that's the case, get out of the marriage and move on. Stop placing the blame and forgive and forget whenever it's possible. When couples cling to their resentment, it's the kids who suffer." She gave an apologetic smile. "Sorry. I didn't mean to get on my soapbox."

"No problem. It's obviously something you feel strongly about."

"If you saw as many kids as I have whose loyalty is torn between their parents, and see what tremendous pressure they're under, you'd feel strongly about it, too."

The coffee sputtered, signaling that it was finished dripping, and Sophie poured two mugs full. "How about bacon and pancakes?"

"Sounds great," Justine said, her stomach growling at the thought.

Sophie got the cast-iron skillet from the stove drawer and took the bacon from the refrigerator.

"I'm going to take a quick shower while you're cooking, if that's okay."

"Go ahead."

"What about Donovan and Lara?" Justine asked when she returned fifteen minutes later, her hair a tumult of wet, dark-red curls. She'd put on a dress in black and taupe that looked good on her, and added color to her lips and eyelashes.

"Better than even Reed and I, if that's possible." Sophie explained to Justine about Lara's indecision to commit to a relationship with Donovan before he'd been arrested in a rape case a few weeks back.

"Of course they had to let him go after a few hours. The cops just picked him up because one of his company's T-shirts was found at the scene and he'd done jail time," Sophie said. "It made Lara understand that her fears and the last bit of resentment she was clinging to were nothing in the scheme of things. I think she realized that life is too uncertain to take anything for granted and that she should grab all the happiness she could before something takes it away."

"I'm glad for Donovan. He deserves to be happy. How is he taking to being a stepdad?"

"He's a natural, but I've always known that. He was always wonderful with Cassidy."

Thrilled for her cousins' happiness but a little sad because that same happiness seemed destined to pass her by, Justine drew in a deep breath, rested her elbow on the table and her chin in her palm. "So everyone lives happily ever after, huh?"

"Hopefully we can manage to do that with only minor upheavals,'' Sophie said, smiling. ''I guess the only fly in our ointment right now is Rowland.''

''Dr. Hardisty?'' Justine said, recalling Reed's father's attitude at the hospital the previous day. ''It's amazing to me that Reed turned out as well as he has with that jerk for a father.''

''No kidding,'' Sophie said, turning the browning bacon. ''I guess Grace's genes were stronger. Or maybe her influence was.''

''So what is the big man doing to make everyone's lives unbearable?''

''He's furious with Reed for marrying me. I'm just that drunk Hutch Delaney's girl, you know. He hardly acknowledges me in a social situation. I don't care about it for myself, but he treats Cassidy the same way, and she's his grandchild.''

''He'll get over it. It may just take him a while.''

Sophie shook her head. ''I don't know.'' She took the last piece of bacon from the skillet and looked at Justine questioningly. ''Fried or scrambled.''

''Do you have to ask?'' Justine said with a little groan. ''I haven't had fried eggs basted the way Mama did them half a dozen times since I left Lewiston.''

''Basted it is.'' Sophie broke two eggs into the hot fat, lowered the heat and began to slosh the drippings over the tops of the eggs. ''You want to make the toast?''

''Sure.''

In minutes they were both at the table, their breakfast in front of them. ''I don't indulge in bacon and eggs often,'' Sophie said, looking down at the two soft-fried eggs with a combination of longing and dismay. ''When I do, the guilt is incredible.''

''Forget the guilt,'' Justine said, spearing another

forkful. "Just enjoy." She ate another bite and said, "Oh, my gosh. These are to die for."

Sophie gave a wry smile. "Exactly."

They both laughed, and Justine pointed her fork at Sophie's plate. "Eat."

They did. Every bite. They even mopped up the runny yellow with their toast. "I don't think you're going to even have to wash my plate, it's so clean," Justine said.

"Mine, either."

Justine got up to warm her coffee. "I can't remember when I've enjoyed food so much."

"There's nothing like home cooking. Or sharing a meal with family." Justine sat down and Sophie reached across the table and took her hand. "I've missed you, Juss."

Justine felt the tears prickle beneath her eyelids. "I've missed you, too. All of you."

"Then why have you kept us at arm's length?"

Justine lifted her tormented gaze to Sophie's. "It's…complicated."

"It always is," Sophie said, adding, "I want to help, Justine."

Justine regarded her cousin's face. Concern and earnest entreaty shone in her eyes. "Can we talk about it another time?"

She gave Justine's hand a pat. "Of course we can."

"After the funeral tomorrow. I promise."

"What about the baby?" Sophie asked. "Can we talk about the baby?"

A wary expression entered Justine's eyes, and her smile was stiff and tight. "That depends on what you want to know."

"Girl or boy?"

"I don't know. For some reason I didn't want to find out."

"Which do you want?"

"It doesn't matter. I just want it."

Sophie smiled. "Do you love him?"

Justine's startled gaze met Sophie's. The loaded question, following so quickly on the heels of the innocent ones, caught her by surprise, eliminating the chance of a carefully thought-out reply. "Yes," she said. Then nodded and said again, "Yes, I do."

"Good, because I can't shake the feeling that the guy feels something for you, too."

Justine's surprise deepened. Sophie knew it was Wes! Or did she? Had she put two and two together, or was she just fishing? "So you think you know who it is, huh?"

"It's Wes, of course," Sophie said without the slightest hesitation. "The tension was so thick between the two of you, you could cut it with a knife."

Justine stared at her cousin in near panic. Had everyone noticed? Probably. None of the people who'd shared the Delaney dinner table were slow-witted.

Hoping to derail Sophie's assumption, Justine said sharply, "Wes's pointed questions could cause tension between two people on tranquilizers."

"Point taken, but I still think I'm right. And if I am, you may as well admit it."

"Why?"

"To ease your mind. To share your load."

"Always the shrink," Justine said with a laugh and a shake of her head.

"Always your cousin and your friend," Sophie corrected.

Justine drew in a deep breath and let it out on a soft

sigh of resignation. "Okay. You're right. It is Wes. He came to my dressing room when I was in Chicago, asked me up to his suite for dinner, and it just... happened."

"That wasn't so hard, was it?" Sophie asked with a smile.

"On the contrary, sweet cousin, it was harder than you'll ever know," Justine told her.

"Well, it certainly explains a lot of things."

"Like what?"

"Like why Wes has been such a bear since then. Like why he's working himself into the ground and why he isn't having much luck with his painting."

Justine looked surprised and amazed. "How do you know all that?"

"My husband is his law partner, remember?"

"Are you saying that the time we spent together has something to do with his current frame of mind?"

"What else could it be?"

Justine didn't know, but to imagine that she could influence Wes's moods in any way was to entertain the idea that she was on his mind, which was ludicrous. Or was it? They'd shared something very special in their youth, before she'd left him without a word of explanation. More than lovers, they'd become friends—two people from differently dysfunctional families who'd discovered something in each other that they'd needed. Was it so ridiculous to imagine that he remembered that time fondly? Was it far-fetched to hope that the night they'd spent together in Chicago had been as memorable for him as it had been for her?

"You slept with him back then, too, didn't you?" Sophie asked.

"Of course I did. You know that."

"You never said, but I suspected," Sophie said. "And it was special, really special, wasn't it?"

Tears filled Justine's eyes. She nodded. "But it wasn't the sex. It was—" she shrugged "—I don't know…the way he made me feel. He always treated me like a lady, Sophie. As if I were his equal, even though we came from vastly different worlds."

"Did you leave because you didn't think anything could come of it?"

Oh, Sophie was clever, Justine thought. Start on one conversation and gradually work your way to another. The temptation to tell her what she wanted to know burned strongly inside Justine. Sophie and Donovan were right. It was time she told someone. Time to see if telling would absolve her of some of the guilt she'd been carrying around for so long—if not the guilt, then maybe she could rid herself of some of the anger and resentment.

She opened her mouth to give Sophie her reason for leaving, but the telephone rang before she could.

"I'll get it," Sophie said, rising. She picked up the receiver with a bright "Hello," listened a second then said, "Oh, hi, Molly. Yes. She's here."

Sophie covered the mouthpiece with her hand and said, "Molly wants to know if you want to meet her at the house."

"No!" Justine said in a sharp voice. She couldn't bear to go back to that house just now. "Ask her to come here."

Sophie relayed the message, told her younger cousin she couldn't wait to see her and said she'd fix her some breakfast when she arrived and hung up.

"Molly said she'd be here in a few minutes," Sophie said. She pointed a finger at Justine. "But don't think you're getting out of that talk. All you've done is post-pone it.''

Justine nodded. There was a lot of that going around.

When Molly arrived thirty minutes later, Justine was amazed by the changes in her young half sister since the last time she'd seen her. How long had it been? Two years? Three? Telling herself that she'd sent regular checks to help Molly through college didn't assuage the guilt that seemed to grow stronger every minute since she'd come back.

Molly, who looked like an all-American nineteen-year-old in her bell-bottom jeans and short shirt that left her belly button showing was clearly surprised by the changes in Justine, too. Justine reminded herself that she'd never told her mother about the baby. Now, sud-denly, she wondered if she should have told her. Maybe knowing she was going to be a grandmother would have given her a tiny bit of pleasure during her last weeks of life. Justine's sorrow and remorse deepened. She ex-changed a perfunctory hug with Molly and felt the stiff-ness in her sister she always felt when they were to-gether, and invisible barrier that even their mutual sorrow couldn't penetrate. It was going to be a long few days.

Holding Molly at arm's length, Justine said, ''You look really good, little sister.''

Molly smiled, a smile that looked just like—whose? Justine wondered. Before she could make the connec-tion, Sophie added her praise of Molly's looks and the moment passed. In a few seconds it was forgotten.

As promised, Sophie fixed breakfast for Molly, and the cousins sat around talking while she ate and then helped clean up the kitchen. They learned that Molly had landed a job doing fashion advertising for one of the more exclusive boutiques in Dallas.

"So Justine isn't the only talented one in the family," Sophie said.

"Guess not." Molly tucked a wayward swathe of coffee-brown hair behind her ear, and Justine felt another of those momentous brink-of-discovery moments flit through her mind.

"Well, I should go," Sophie said with a sigh. "I know you two have a lot to talk about. But I've enjoyed it. Maybe now that I'm closer, we can see more of each other," Sophie said. "You're coming back here for the holidays, and summer, aren't you, Molly?"

"I'm not sure," Molly hedged. "With Mama gone, I don't really have anything or anyone to come home to. I know she left the place to me, because she knew Justine wouldn't want it, and I'm thinking of selling."

The thought of Molly selling her old home didn't bother Justine at all, yet another shard of guilt pierced her heart at the notion that Molly felt alone. "Why don't you come to Nashville and spend the holidays with me?" she offered. "Christmas, at least."

"Actually, my boyfriend and his family asked me to spend Christmas with them," Molly said without meeting her sister's gaze.

Justine was surprised at the depth of her disappointment. "Oh. Well, if you change your mind, just let me know."

"Sure."

Knowing the sisters had much to discuss, Sophie said her goodbyes, and Justine and Molly waved her off from Donovan's front porch.

"It's nice out here," Justine said, drawing in a deep breath of the clean country air.

"We can stay out here if you want," Molly said.

"Let's do."

Molly chose the swing, tucking her feet up under her, while Justine sat in the rocker. "When is the baby due?" Molly asked.

Justine met Molly's gaze but volunteered no more than she was asked. "The middle of November."

"I read in one of the country music magazines that you were pregnant, but sometimes you never know what to believe."

"Well, in this case they were right."

"Have you been feeling okay?" Molly asked, genuine concern in her eyes.

"I was deathly ill at first, twenty-four hours of the day, seven days a week. But the past few months have been okay. Look, can we talk about something else?"

Molly stiffened visibly, and Justine wished she could take back the request.

"I'm sorry," Molly said. "I didn't mean to pry."

"No." Justine said, reaching out and covering her sister's hand with one of her own. "I'm sorry. You weren't prying. It's just that this is one subject I'm not comfortable talking about."

"I understand."

They sat in silence for several minutes. Donovan drove up and parked near the greenhouses, then sauntered over and joined them.

"It looks natural to see the two of you sitting out here," he said, coming up the steps and leaning against a post. "Women and porches just seem to go together."

"Mama and Aunt Ruby spent a lot of time on their front porches, didn't they?" Justine asked.

Donovan and Molly nodded. Molly's brown eyes held a faraway expression. "Seems like they were always peeling peaches or snapping beans or shucking corn.'' Justine saw the glimmer of tears in her eyes. ''She worked so hard.''

''Yes, she did,'' Justine said. ''They both did. But they had fun, too.''

''It's because they were so close,'' Molly said. ''They both had terrible home lives, but they took a comfort and what joy they could in the time they spent together.''

The statement surprised Justine, first that her younger sister had been aware of the shortcomings in her father that led to the terrible state of her home life, and second by her insight to the special bond between their mother and their aunt.

''Sophie said she cooked breakfast,'' Donovan said. ''Is there anything left?''

''Not cooked,'' Justine told him, already rising. ''But I'd be glad to fix you some.''

''Sit down. I'm a big boy, and I've been taking care of myself for a long time. You girls sit and visit.'' He disappeared into the house.

After a few moments of silence, Justine asked, ''Are the boys coming to the funeral?''

Her stepbrothers, Duke and Joe Bob, were Gene's boys by his first wife, whose story was the stereotypical stuff of redneck jokes. She'd run off with a traveling tool salesman, leaving Gene with two small boys. Justine had often heard her own mother say that Gene had only married her to get a baby-sitter, and Justine believed it. She never had understood why her mother, whose first husband—Justine's dad—had been a good, hardworking man, had married someone who was so clearly a loser.

''I doubt it. I never hear from them, either, so I don't

even know where they are,'' Molly said, then shot a glance at Justine when she realized that the statement could be construed as critical. ''I didn't mean—''

Justine shook her head. ''That's what Sophie would call a Freudian slip. And don't apologize. It's okay. I haven't kept in touch the way I should, and you have every right to resent me for that. Mama told me one day I'd be sorry, and if it's any consolation I am.''

Molly's eyes glazed with tears, and she sat there, clearly struggling to find the right words to express herself. Justine searched her own mind for something to ease the awkwardness of the moment. Molly excused herself and went inside. Justine was struggling with her own emotions when she heard the sound of a car coming down the lane.

Donovan came out onto the porch carrying a bacon sandwich as the car, an antique roadster came into view.

''Someone must be bringing food,'' Justine said.

Donovan took a big bite of his sandwich and said, ''That's Wes.''

Justine had to grip the arms of the rocking chair to keep from getting up and running inside to hide.

As the car pulled in front of the porch, Justine realized there were two people inside. A feeling of relief swept through her. There was little chance of Wes asking any personal questions if someone was with him. A closer look told her the passenger was a woman, an older woman. Only when she opened the car and got out did Justine recognize Wes's companion as his great-aunt, Isabelle Duncan, the richest, most eccentric person in town.

It was Isabelle who had stood up for Donovan to the bank's board when he'd applied for the money to put in his business and renovate the house. The board, who at first hadn't wanted to lend money to an ex-convict, had agreed to the loan readily enough when Isabelle threatened to pull her considerable millions. Everyone knew that a threat from Isabelle was as good as it being a done deal.

Molly, once more in control of her emotions, came back outside. "Good grief," she said. "Is that who I think it is?"

"It is if you think it's Isabelle Duncan."

"And Wes Grayson," Molly murmured appreciatively. "What a hunk."

"Yeah," Justine said with a sad little smile. What on earth was Wes doing driving Isabelle around? Where was her driver and her Bentley? She was glad suddenly that she'd taken time to put on at least a little makeup earlier and that the dress she was wearing was one that looked good on her...at least as good as she could look with no figure. She knew her hair had dried to its usual curliness, and while it might not be stylish, it wasn't unattractive. It was the best she could hope for.

Despite her years, Isabelle exited the car with an ease Justine envied, clutching a casserole dish in a padded cover in both hands. As usual Isabelle's dress was at least sixty years out of style. Amazingly, she was able to carry the classy forties style off with a certain flair, partly, Justine thought, because she was still able to fit into it.

"Hello, my dears," Isabelle said with a smile.

"Hello, Miss Isabelle." Justine, Molly and Donovan chimed together as Isabelle made her way up the steps. Justine noticed that Wes was busy getting something else from the back seat. She dreaded having to face him.

"Justine, you look just as marvelous as your publicity photos," Isabelle commented, turning her cheek upward for a kiss from Donovan, who complied as if he'd done it often. Without waiting for an answer, she turned to Molly. "And you, young lady, have turned into a gorgeous thing."

"Thank you, Miss Isabelle," Molly said. "Would you like to sit down?"

"Yes, thank you."

"Let me take that," Justine offered, reaching for the casserole dish.

"Thank you, my dear. I wasn't sure how many people were coming, so I made my Mexican casserole, a coconut cake and fried chicken." She glanced at Wes, who was carrying a large Tupperware cake carrier and a foil-covered platter up the steps. "Just follow Justine," Isabelle told him in a tone that said she was accustomed to being obeyed.

"Yes, ma'am."

"Need some help, Counselor?" Donovan asked with a wide grin, a teasing expression in his blue eyes.

"I can manage, thanks," Wes said shortly.

Justine felt his eyes on her as he followed her inside, but in spite of the situation, she found herself smiling at the thought of Wes meekly taking orders from anyone. She set the dish on the counter. When Wes put his things next to hers and glanced her way, she was still smiling.

A reluctant grin claimed his lips. For a moment there was no complicated past between them, no uncertain future, just the openness they'd felt as kids. They were just two people marveling at the abilities of an old woman.

"She's tough," he said, shaking his head.

"She's priceless."

He nodded. "That, too."

Justine scoured her mind for something else to say. Wes seemed at a loss for words, too, and an awkward silence grew between them.

"Don't forget to put the cake in the refrigerator!" Isabelle called from the porch.

Justine, who'd been staring into Wes's fathomless dark eyes and wondering what he was thinking, jumped. "Yes, ma'am!" she said. "I'll do it right now."

Thankful for the reprieve, she brushed past Wes and picked up the cake. When she turned toward the refrigerator, she saw that he'd taken the request as an opportunity to escape. Thank goodness. Still, she couldn't stay inside. There was nothing to do but go out and join the others.

"You'll like the cake," Isabelle was saying as Justine stepped back outside. "It's your aunt Ruby's recipe." She turned to Justine. "Sit there on the swing by Weston, Justine."

Justine's gaze flew to his, but he only smiled politely and scooted over. Good manners prohibited her declining, so she settled into the space next to him. Good manners also dictated that she offer them some refreshment. "Would you like something to drink, Miss Isabelle?"

"Not just now, thank you. Weston?"

Wes began to move the swing back and forth. "I'm fine."

"I was telling Molly that my driver is sick," Isabelle said. "Some flu bug or something. So I called Wes, and he graciously offered to bring me out here." Isabelle laughed, a deep rusty sound. "He refused to drive the Bentley, but I must say the roadster rides pretty well."

Donovan and Wes exchanged amused glances, and

Donovan said, "I hate to leave good company, but I have some work to do, if you'll excuse me."

"By all means," Isabelle said. "Don't let us keep you." She gave him a denture-filled smile. "I don't suppose you'd have time to show me around, would you? So I can report back to the bank board."

"You want to see how I spent your money, huh?" Donovan said, smiling. "I don't blame you. Sure. I'd be glad to give you the grand tour." He glanced at the others. "Do you all want to go?"

"No thanks," Justine said. "I'm still not feeling 100 percent."

"I'd love to go," Molly said, rising.

"You all go on," Wes said, glancing from Donovan to Justine. He smiled that sexy half smile that set her heart aflutter. "I'll stay here and keep Justine company."

Chapter Four

Alone with Wes, Justine thought. Just what she needed. Still, there was nothing to do but muddle through the next few minutes as best she could and hope she wasn't forced into a corner about the baby's paternity.

"Are you feeling better?"

"Yes, thank you," Justine said in a prim voice.

"I'm sorry about your mother."

Justine glanced over at Wes in surprise. She hadn't expected the conversation to run to condolences. Confrontations, yes.

"I was so young when mine died that I don't remember much about her. I do remember that it was lonely, though. The two of you weren't close, were you?"

She fought the urge to cry. She refused to meet his questioning gaze, refused to be drawn into a discussion about her relationship with her mother...especially with Wes Grayson. ''No.''

''That's too bad.''

''Yes.''

''Don't want to talk about it, huh?''

''Not really.''

''Would you rather talk about your baby?''

''There's not much to talk about,'' Justine said, twining her hands together in her lap.

''Are you excited?''

What was he doing? She wondered. She slanted him a sideways glance. ''I believe we discussed this last night before dinner.''

''You're right. We did,'' he acknowledged with a nod. ''And you said the baby is due the middle of November.''

''That's right.''

''Is it a boy or a girl?''

It was a toss-up as to whether Justine wanted to scream in frustration or get up and run inside away from him and his questions. She wondered how she could have felt so comfortable with him a few months before, that they'd shared the most intimate of acts, yet felt so awkward with him now.

''Is it mine?''

She sucked in a sharp breath. Wes was known for his no-nonsense approach to interrogation, but until now, she'd had no idea just how pointed his questions could be. Her twined hands tightened on each other. Lying wasn't her style, but now that she was faced with the opportunity to tell him the truth, she wasn't sure she could. She'd already thought about the various scenarios that might occur if she told him the baby was his, and none of them was palatable. She forced herself to breathe normally, to look him in the eye when she answered.

"Why would you even think such a thing?" she asked, thinking that he had the most gorgeous eyes and wondering if he'd pass that trait on to their child.

"I did the math."

Her gaze slid from his to the greenhouses across the way. "Well, yes, I see your point, but you aren't the only man in the world."

"So you were sleeping with someone else when you spent the night with me?"

No, I wasn't. Justine didn't answer.

"Do you do that often?" There was a hint of steel in his voice.

"Do what often?" she asked, frowning.

"Sleep with two men at once."

"No," she snapped. "Never."

"Do you love him?"

"I beg your pardon?" Justine asked, aghast at his directness.

"Do you love this other guy?"

You're getting in deeper and deeper, Justine. "If you're asking if I love the man who fathered my baby, the answer is yes, I do. Very much."

"If you've never cheated on him, then why this time? Why me?"

Justine had taken about all she could. Her nerves were stretched to the breaking point, and she wasn't sure how long she could hold back the tears. She pushed herself to her feet and went to the porch railing, clinging to it like a shipwrecked sailor latches on to a piece of flotsam. "What do you want from me?" she asked without looking at him.

She heard the chains of the swing creak, heard him

take the two steps it took to reach her. She closed her eyes, as if by doing so she could deny his closeness. Impossible. She felt his presence, felt the heat of his body close to hers and the warmth of his breath as he spoke close to her ear.

"Some answers would be nice."

"I've answered all your questions."

"Most of them," he agreed. "But you never said why, Justine. If you were involved with someone else, why did you agree to go to my room?"

"Why did you ask me to?" she countered, taking refuge in a counterattack, turning to face him in defiance. "Why did you come to the concert? Why did you come backstage?"

Wes's eyes darkened with irritation.

"What's the matter, Wes? Why don't you answer me? Third degrees aren't much fun when you're on the receiving end of them, are they?" When he didn't reply, she turned back to the railing, closed her eyes and prayed for the others to return.

"I don't know why I came."

The words were spoken so softly, Justine wondered at first if she'd imagined them. She heard him sigh.

"I saw the ad for the concert on the television and the next thing I knew I was there."

She couldn't respond for the tears clogging her throat and threatening to spill over her eyelashes. He sounded as confused as she'd felt the morning she'd awakened with him sleeping so soundly beside her. She swallowed hard and forced herself to face him again, feigning a bravado she was far from feeling.

"You asked me why you?" she said, "Probably for the same reason you came to the concert. We both wanted to see if there were any sparks left of the old flame. I imagine we've both wondered about that through the years.'' She forced a smile. "So now we know.''

"Yeah,'' he said, plunging his hands into his pockets. "Now we know. Does he?''

"What?'' she asked, not following.

"Does this other guy know about the night we spent together?''

Realizing her sophistry was only getting her in deeper, Justine fell back on irritation. "Who do you think you are, Wes? Just because we shared one night of fantastic sex, you have no right to question me about my other relationships.''

"You're right. Your personal relationships aren't any of my business.''

A sigh of relief trickled from her. Maybe he'd leave her alone now.

"You know, it didn't have to end so suddenly.''

What did he mean? She wondered, searching his eyes for some sign of what he was thinking. Was he talking about Chicago or their youthful love affair?

"There was no place for it to go beyond where we were,'' she said, aware that her comment, too, could be applied to either situation.

He lifted one shoulder in a negligent shrug. "Maybe you're right, but after everything we shared, I expected more. You could have at least said goodbye.''

He was talking about the past, then. Something she couldn't talk about. "Goodbyes have a tendency to get messy.''

"So you just packed up and left.''

She nodded, knowing her blasé attitude made her seem cold and unfeeling and knowing it was for the best. "I just packed up and left.''

"Why?"

Her stomach knotted. Even the baby seemed to draw away from the question, into a small, hard ball. Barely aware of her actions, she put both hands on her belly. "What is this, Wes?" she challenged. "Twenty Questions?"

His dark eyebrows drew together in a frown. "Are you all right?"

His unexpected concern seemed genuine and caught Justine off guard. "Of course I'm all right. Why?"

"You... You're holding your...stomach. I thought you might be in pain."

"It's just Braxton Hicks pains."

"Braxton Hicks pains? What the hell are those?"

"Sort of false labor pains," she said, massaging gently.

Alarm flashed into his eyes. "Labor! How do you know it's false?"

"Because I do."

She realized that somehow in the past few seconds, the thread of emotion between the two of them had lost its tension. His confrontational attitude and her need to be on guard against his personal questions had vanished. The situation held a certain poignance, offering her a glimpse of the kind of husband and father he had the potential to be. Caring. Concerned. A facet of himself he seldom allowed to be seen, preferring to hide any softness beneath a shell of arrogance and sarcasm. Justine knew the shell was as much for protection as it was to put off people.

They stood there for several seconds, each thinking his own thoughts, each wondering what would happen next. "I hated you for a long time after you left," Wes said at last.

"I knew you would."

"It didn't bother you?"

"There was nothing I could do to change it, so I just tried to put it out of my mind."

"Did you?"

"For days at a time, sometimes," she said, nodding. She gave him a soft, self-deprecating smile. "It was for the best, Wes. You know it as well as I do. As I said, our relationship had nowhere to go."

"You don't know that."

"Of course I do. What would you have done? Waited until I graduated and married me?" She shook her head. "I can't see your...father ever agreeing to that."

The expression in his eyes said he knew she had a point. "You could have at least told me you were going."

"As I said, it would just have gotten messy. And I didn't want you to try to talk me out of it or make me feel guilty for what I had to do. And I did have to leave."

She saw the dawning of understanding in his eyes. "You weren't pregnant back then, were you?" he asked. "Is that why you left town?"

"No," she assured him. "I wasn't pregnant. You were very...considerate about birth control, even back then." She smiled a weary sort of smile. "But if I had been, I wouldn't have told you."

"I've never minded owning up to my responsibilities."

"I know." From the corner of her eye, she saw Donovan and the others round the corner of the far greenhouse. "Everyone's coming back. Can we finish this discussion another time?"

"Sure," he said with a curt nod. "Just one thing more."

"What's that?"

"You were right. It was fantastic sex."

In spite of herself, Justine felt her face flame. She was still trying to calm her racing heart when she heard Isabelle's voice floating toward them on a soft breeze.

"...absolutely wonderful. Very impressive."

Desperate for a reprieve, Justine turned and saw Molly trailing behind Isabelle who clumped up the steps, her face glowing with excitement and exertion.

"Donovan has certainly done things right," she said to no one in particular.

"He always does," Justine replied.

"He does, doesn't he?" Isabelle took Justine's hands in hers. "Wes and I must go, my dear, but I wanted to tell you and Molly how very sorry I am about your mother's death. She was a decent, hardworking woman who managed to maintain her dignity even in the hardest of times."

Molly's eyes filled with tears. Feeling near tears herself, Justine squeezed Isabelle's hands. "Thank you."

Isabelle smiled. "How long are you staying?"

"I'm not sure," Justine said, with a shrug. "At least long enough to help Molly get Mama's things squared away."

"A few days, then, at least." Isabelle patted Justine's hand. "Don't be a stranger."

"I won't."

Isabelle held out her arm toward her great-nephew. "Weston."

Wes's glance moved from his aunt to Justine and then Molly before he said his goodbyes and offered his arm to his aunt. Justine watched them go down the steps and get into the car, a feeling of loneliness and despair washing over her.

Lara was watering her backyard plants, which were lagging in the relentless September heat wave, when Wes stopped by later that afternoon. "What are you doing here?"

"What's the matter?" he asked. "Can't I stop by for a visit without you acting like it's a big deal?"

"You could if that was your usual behavior, but since you're the original loner and you just graced us with your company last night, I'm wondering what's up."

"Nothing's up," Wes said, irritably. "I just stopped by to see if I can go with you and Donovan to the funeral home tonight."

"We'd be glad for you to go with us. Visitation is from seven to nine, I believe. We're even having dinner out before we go, if you want to join us."

"Where are you going?"

"Dairy Delight, where else?" Lara said with a smile. "Their steak finger basket is on special today."

"Mmm, yummy," Wes said, rolling his eyes.

"Hey, if you're too good to eat that stuff, you can eat a bologna sandwich at home and meet us at the funeral parlor later."

"I'm not too good to eat fast food. Actually, steak finger baskets used to be one of my favorite things. That and chili cheeseburgers."

"Good." Lara trained the nozzle of the watering wand on the roots of a hibiscus. "Why do you want to tag along with us? You aren't exactly a shy type."

Wes plunged his hands into the pockets of his jeans. "No, but I didn't know Opal Malone all that well."

"True. What was that between you and Justine last night?" Lara asked, casting him a sideways look.

"What was what?" he asked with impeccable nonchalance.

"That third degree you gave her. Just because the two of you dated a couple of times doesn't give you the right to grill her the way you did. And by the way, you promised you'd tell me about your youthful fling sometime, and you haven't."

"I didn't grill her," Wes said, ignoring her last statement. He knew he'd promised, but he wasn't ready to spill his guts to his sister about Justine. "I just asked her some questions."

"Yeah. Some pretty personal questions. In short, you were rude, Wes, and that isn't like you. Blunt, yes. Downright rude, no. Would you like to tell me what's going on?"

"Nothing's going on," he lied. "I just wish you'd have told me she was here before you asked me to go wake her for dinner."

The question in Lara's eyes seemed to ask why. She shrugged. "I'm sorry. With all the company, it slipped my mind."

"Did you know she was pregnant?"

"Yeah." She swung the watering wand in slow, back and forth strokes. "I saw it on one of the country music channels."

"Why didn't you tell me?"

Lara looked at him strangely. "Because, brother dear, it never occurred to me that you'd want to know. Why would you want to know, unless..." Her eyes widened and she stood stock-still. "Wait a minute. Was this date you had with Justine when she was in high school more than a date?"

Wes knew it was time to fess up. Lara had scented blood, and he knew she wouldn't leave him alone until he told all. What the heck, he thought. Why not just tell her what she wanted to know and get it over with. It was old news, anyway. "And if it was?"

"If it was more...if intimacy was involved, I'd say that you still have no right to use your gestapo methods on her. You were just kids. It's over and has been for a long time."

"No, it isn't."

Lara blinked in disbelief. "Isn't what? Isn't over? What are you talking about?"

"What if I told you I saw her in Chicago?"

"I'd ask you to be more specific about what *saw* means."

Wes gave an elegant, negligent shrug. "We spent some time together."

"I assume you weren't playing Scrabble," she said in a voice that bordered on sarcasm.

"You'd assume right."

"Dear God, Wes!" Lara said, not even trying to mask her shock.

"Would you please be more specific about what Dear God means?" he asked.

"It means I can't believe it. I can't believe that you and Justine Sutton... I mean, you can have your pick of women."

"Are you implying there's something wrong with Justine? If so, I'd remind you that you just married her cousin."

"I'm not implying anything of the kind. But she's in Nashville, and you're here. What made you decide to look her up after so many years?"

"I wish I knew."

"It wasn't that Donovan and I and Sophie and Reed were rediscovering each other and you felt—I don't know—left out or something, was it?"

"Think about it Lara. Chicago was seven months ago. Donovan and Sophie didn't come until four months later."

Lara chewed on her lower lip thoughtfully. "Oh. Right."

"You're making a puddle."

"What?"

Wes gestured toward Lara's feet, where the watering wand had deposited a fair amount of water since he'd sprung the news about him and Justine.

"Darn!" Her feet squashing wetly in her shoes, she went to turn off the water. As she bent to turn off the faucet, she froze. "Oh...my...gosh," she said in a horrified voice.

"What?" Wes demanded, sprinting toward her, afraid that she'd run into a snake or something. As he approached her, Lara straightened and grabbed his arm, her eyes wide. "What?" he asked again.

"You were asking Justine all those questions about the baby because you think it's yours, don't you?"

"The time frame is right for it to be a possibility, but the lady assured me that I'm way off base."

"She did?" Lara frowned. "She actually told you there was another man in her life?"

Wes thought back to his conversation with Justine. What had she said? *"...you aren't the only man in the world, Wes."*

Not exactly naming names, was she? And when he'd asked her outright if she was sleeping with someone else, she'd said...what?

She didn't answer, Grayson. Wes felt his stomach

churn. When he'd asked her if she often slept with two
men, she'd said no, never. Damn! She hadn't admitted
to a thing. All she'd done was to lead him down the
path he'd wanted to be taken down. Now, realizing that
he'd fallen for her misdirection, he felt a hollowness
inside him. Why had she done it?

"Wes?" Lara prompted. "What did she tell you?"

"Actually, she didn't admit to seeing someone else,
she just got on the defensive and asked me questions
and said things to make me think she was."

"Well, there's one way to find out, if you really want
to know."

"Of course I want to know," he said in exasperation.
"But how can you find out?"

"Easy. I'll ask Sophie if Justine was seeing anyone
back in February."

"And you actually think she'll tell you?"

"Why wouldn't she?" Lara asked. "I don't have to
tell her why I want to know." She gave his arm a sis-
terly pat. "I'm a smart girl, Wes. I can do this so she
won't suspect a thing."

"Then do it."

"What will you do when you find out? What if it is
your baby?"

Wes scraped a hand through his hair. "I don't
know."

"Do you know what I find the hardest to believe?"

"What?"

"That neither of you took care of birth control. I
mean, it isn't as if you're teenagers who don't know
the score."

"For your information, we did use birth control," he
growled. "As long as it lasted."

Lara laughed, and a soft blush tinted her cheeks.

"Whoa! Too much information." She looped her arm through his and hugged it. "What about Justine? Do you think what you feel for her is lasting, or is it just physical?"

"It's more than physical. It always was. She understood the way Dad made me feel."

"Join the crowd."

Wes took a step back. "What do you mean? Oh, no," he said, when Lara raised an eyebrow. "It's not what you think. I'm not in love with her."

"Then why haven't you married any of those other women who tried to get you to the altar? Why haven't you ever slipped up on birth control before?"

"Are you saying that was deliberate?"

"All I'm saying is that you need to give some thought about what it is you really feel for Justine and what it is you want if she is carrying your baby. This can either be a wonderful thing, or something ugly. It will depend on how the two of you handle it."

A picture flashed in his mind of Justine in the kitchen of the cabin, a toddler clinging to her leg…of himself carrying a laughing little boy on his shoulders down to the lake, the sleeping child resting trustingly in the crook of his arm, the other arm around Justine. The scenario held a certain appeal.

Yeah. But cute is one thing and responsibility is another. A wife is going to demand things…

Things like fidelity. Sharing thoughts and feelings and dreams and disappointments. Well, the first part was easy. He couldn't even imagine making love to another woman. As for the sharing, it wasn't going to be easy after all these years, but Justine understood the creative mind…surely he could make it work.

What are you thinking, Grayson? Surely you aren't

contemplating marriage. Doing right by the baby is something, but a wife, now, that's something else.

Wes ignored the voice. He'd have to see what happened between him and Justine, but there was no way he could not participate in his child's life. His innate sense of right and wrong dictated that, at least.

All these happy thoughts about you and bonding with a kid is cute, but don't forget that a baby is going to get sick. It's also going to get into things…like your paints…and your African tribal mask collection.

But what if he or she inherited his artistic bent, or Justine's musical ability? The other part of him, the part that was weary of being alone and lonely, argued its case. That would be awesome. But then, just knowing that he and Justine had created a child from the most basic of acts, was awesome.

Nothing basic about what the two of you shared. More like something out of time, something awesome in and of itself. Something so fantastic it was downright…

"Scary, isn't it?"

"What?" he asked, coming back to earth in a rush.

"The thought that you have the prospect of being a parent. A father."

"Yeah," he said. "It's scary." He looked at his sister, the expression in his eyes both frightened and determined. "I've got to go. Give Sophie a call, will you?"

Justine and Molly didn't have much time for talking or getting to know each other better after Isabelle and Wes left. They set the time of the funeral for ten the next morning. It wasn't the way either of them wanted to start the week, but since they were the only close family coming from out of town, there was no sense putting it off.

The remainder of Sunday was spent receiving visitors, talking about the old days—a lot of "do you remember whens" and "I remember the times." And there was the food, more food than she and Molly and all the visitors could possibly eat...enough food to feed the homeless in Lewiston for a week. In fact, she'd mentioned to the minister who was presiding over the funeral that that's what she and Molly wanted to do with it.

Justine had been dreading visitation time. It was one thing to be in familiar surroundings, talking about old times, sharing memories and even laughter, and another to be in the formal setting of the funeral home and watch those who wanted to view her mother's body and pay their last respects parade by in hushed reverence and then stop somberly by where she and Molly sat and say they were sorry.

As hard as it was to do, Justine did it. It was the least she could do for her mother, no matter what the situation had been between them. She was surprised at the number of people who had stopped by Donovan's house and were now coming into the small room wearing their Sunday clothes and solemn faces.

Clearly, she thought, as she accepted another offer of sympathy, her mother had been well liked. As well she should have been, because both she and her twin sister, Ruby, Sophie's mother, had been good, likeable people at heart. They'd just happened to have had poor judgment and ended up with two men who were the scum of the earth.

Justine remembered the whispers as she was growing up and realized that she was not only poor, she was looked down on for it. Regardless, her mother had always expected a certain behavior from them. They were required to say "ma'am" and "sir," to show respect to others and not deface others' property. They were taught to show respect for the world and the creatures God created, do their best in school and go to church on Sunday. At least they did until her mama married Gene Malone.

Justine pushed the thought of Gene from her mind and murmured, "Thank you for coming."

How many times had she said those words in the past hour? she wondered. But even as she made the accepted responses, her conversation with Wes was never far from her thoughts. Had her misdirection and defensive tactics worked? Had she convinced him that he wasn't the only man in her life during the time the baby was conceived? She hoped so.

For all his eccentricity, Wes Grayson was, in many ways, a very traditional Southern male. He believed in protecting women, not in exploiting them. He believed in taking responsibility for his actions, so it followed that *if* he found out for sure the baby was his, he'd want to do something about it. Justine was afraid that that something might be a demand to be part of their child's life.

She could live with that. With them residing in different states, it would be hard, but it was workable. What she couldn't live with was the thought that Wes might use his money and influence to get custody of their baby. But Wes wasn't like that—was he?

Then, almost as if her thoughts had somehow conjured him up, he stepped through the door behind Donovan, Lara, Cassidy and Belle. Despite her fears, her sorrow and her fatigue, Justine's heart reacted as it typically did to him. It seemed to stumble, stop and then start racing, like a Thoroughbred out of a gate. A part of her had expected him to come; another part argued that he had come to the house with Isabelle earlier, so there was no need.

Their eyes met as he followed the others to the open casket. The expression in his seemed guarded, questioning. Her cousin and his new family didn't tarry at the casket, swiftly moving to her instead. Justine saw tears in Donovan's eyes as he pulled her to her feet and into his arms.

She clung to him while he choked out, "She looks so much like Mama, it's like losing her all over again."

Indeed, Justine, thought, that's probably how it did seem, looking at Ruby's twin. Sophie would no doubt feel the same way. Donovan released her and moved to Molly. Justine accepted a hug from Lara, who said, "She looks very nice."

Justine bit her lip and nodded before accepting hugs from Cassidy and Belle. From the whiteness of Belle's face, Justine guessed it was her first encounter with death. They moved past Justine, and she found herself staring up into Wes's eyes.

"I need to talk to you."

Justine gasped. No condolences. No display of sorrow. Only a demand, which was accompanied by an expression in his eyes that told her he expected her to comply.

"I think we said everything there was to say this morning," she told him in a low voice.

"Not quite."

From the corner of her eye, Justine saw some other people approaching. The last thing she needed was to have the fact that she and Wes were arguing at her mother's visitation spread all over town. "Now isn't a good time, Wes."

"I know that," he said, his voice low and borderline irritated. "I'll be outside when this is over. Have Donovan take Molly home."

And what did he expect her to tell everyone about the reason she was staying behind to talk to him? "No," she said. "I can't do that. People would talk."

He nodded. "Right. Call me when you get home."

He moved away toward Molly, leaving Justine feeling frustrated and angry and a little scared. Whatever it was he had to say, he meant to say it. What did he want now?

Chapter Five

Justine and Molly drove home from the funeral parlor in Justine's Mustang that Donovan had fetched from the hospital parking lot and brought to the house earlier that day. Like her, Molly was exhausted, but not too exhausted to admire the car.

"Great wheels."

"Thanks," Justine said. "But it isn't what one needs if you belong to the car-seat set, though. I guess it's time to move up into something bigger."

"That's a shame."

"Well, you know what Mama always said, 'If you want to dance, you have to pay the fiddler.'" She smiled at Molly. "I guess the price of getting pregnant is being forced to give up your Mustang for a minivan."

"Eek!" Molly said in horror.

Justine smiled. "Exactly."

She dropped Molly off at the house where they'd

both grown up, knowing that the time was rapidly approaching when she'd have to force herself to go inside and deal with the memories.

"I'll see you in the morning," Justine said. "What time did the funeral director say they'd pick us up?"

"About nine."

"See you then," Justine said with a nod. "Sleep well."

"I'm so exhausted, I'll probably crash," Molly said.

"Me, too. Good night."

"'Night." Justine waited until Molly was safely inside, then drove to Donovan's. Inside, she took a hot shower to relax, brushed her teeth and changed into a knee-length, vee-necked gown of teal satin, all the while trying not to think of what it might be that Wes wanted to talk to her about this time. She stifled a yawn as she made her way to the kitchen to turn off the lights. Whatever it was could darn well wait until tomorrow. She had no intention of calling him when she was so bone weary.

She got a drink of water, turned off the lights and groped her way down the hallway to the room she'd chosen to sleep in…the one Cassidy had claimed while she and Sophie stayed at the house.

The bed felt wonderful. The mattress was just right, and the sheets were cool to the touch. The baby moved, as if he, too, was ready to get settled in for the night. She closed her eyes and tried to empty her mind of everything—disturbing memories of the past, flashes of conversation she'd had about her mother with different people throughout the day, dread for the task that lay ahead the following day and worries about what it might be that Wes wanted.

She drew in a deep, contented breath and smelled the

incomparable scent of lavender. Sophie's touch, no doubt. Justine hoped the herb did its work. She concentrated on relaxing—tensing then loosening the muscles of her feet first, then her legs, moving up her body until she was certain her body was at rest beneath the light quilt that, despite the warm daytime temperatures, she knew she'd need before morning.

An owl hooted outside and, from the kitchen, Justine heard the clatter of the ice maker emptying ice cubes and refilling with water. The sound of an approaching car drifted to her on the silence of the night. She tensed. It was barely 10 p.m., but who on earth would come calling so late? Someone who'd missed visitation?

She pushed the button on the bedside lamp, got up and donned the robe that matched her gown. She turned on the kitchen and porch lights and peeked out the window. She had no intention of opening the door to strangers at this hour of the night, no matter why they were coming. She didn't know whether to be relieved or angry when she recognized the car belonged to Wes.

She swung the door open as he came up the steps. "What are you doing here at this time of night?" she asked, without bothering to hide her irritation.

"I told you I needed to talk."

Crossing her arms over her middle, she said, "I'm tired, Wes. Can't it wait?"

"Maybe. But I'm not a patient type of guy."

"I noticed." He didn't seem angry, she thought, only determined. That was good. Maybe she was worrying for nothing. Torn between weariness, exasperation and a nagging anxiety, she sighed heavily and stepped out of the doorway. "You may as well come in."

"Thank you," he said with all the graciousness her invitation lacked.

"Would you like something to drink?"

"No, thanks. I've already had so much caffeine I'm about to jump out of my skin."

"Fine." She gestured toward the table with one hand and the casual living-room seating in front of the fireplace with the other. "Where would you like to sit?"

Wes headed for the sofa. "This is good," he said, taking a seat on the sofa.

Her stomach churning with dread, Justine sat down in an armchair across from him and refolded her arms. She was relatively certain that whatever it was he'd come to say, she didn't want to hear it.

"I've thought a lot about what you said earlier—or rather what you didn't say," he told her.

"And what didn't I say?"

"When I asked you if there was another man, you never really said yes."

Justine's heart took a nosedive.

"You talked all around the subject, changed the subject and came back with some questions to take my mind off my question. So I started thinking…and I talked with Lara, and—"

"You talked with your sister about me?" Justine's voice was just below a shriek.

"She knows something's up between us, Justine. Everyone does."

"How could they?" she asked, jumping to her feet with more energy than grace. "*I* certainly haven't said anything. I haven't even told Sophie we saw each other in Chicago."

"I told Lara."

Shocked, unable to believe what she was hearing, Justine stared at him, speechless. She'd guarded the secret of her child's paternity as closely as if national security depended on it, and now Wes, Mr. Cool and Unflappable, was blabbing it all over town.

"She was already suspicious because of the way I grilled you at dinner last night."

"I *knew* they'd get suspicious!" Justine paced to the kitchen area and back again. "Your questions were pretty pointed for a casual observer."

"Evidently. Anyway, she asked what was going on, and I told her."

"Told her? Told her what?" Justine cried.

"That we'd spent some time together in Chicago, and that the baby might be mine."

"Sweet heaven!" Justine breathed with a shake of her head. "Who else have you told?"

"Reed."

"Why didn't you just take out a full-page ad in the *Ledger*," Justine said, mentioning Lewiston's small weekly newspaper. "You know, something with a headline along the lines of I Slept with Justine Sutton in Chicago in February." She held her hands up as if she were framing an imaginary page of print. "Maybe the subtitle could be Her Baby May Be Mine. Then you could fill in the rest with all the juicy details."

"So you admit it."

"Admit what?" she asked, knowing she'd let her tongue run away with her. She also knew she'd taken her defensive stance about as far as she could. Any minute now Wes was bound to turn the tables on her and demand to know the answers to his questions.

"The baby could be mine."

"It isn't."

"How sure are you?"

"Sure enough."

"I'm not," he said, his sharp dark gaze probing hers.

Why couldn't he leave well enough alone? she wondered, rubbing at her aching temples with her fingertips. Why couldn't he accept her answer that the baby wasn't his and go on with his life? Knowing she was in for a rough time and not certain she could cope with it, she pushed her tousled auburn hair away from her face with a weary gesture. "Look, Wes, we've been through all this."

"You're right, but this time I'd appreciate it if you'd give me some straight answers."

"Fine," she snapped. "Exactly what is it you want to know?"

"Who's the other man?"

Justine knew her back was against the proverbial wall. Maybe she could turn the tables one more time. "What do you want?" she countered with studied sarcasm. "His name and phone number?"

"Why not?" Wes shot back, clearly losing patience with her and her prevaricating. "Since you won't say anything, maybe he and I can compare notes and get to the bottom of this."

Fuming, Justine turned her back on him and went into the kitchen. She got herself a glass of water and turned, leaning her back against the cabinets. Irritation glittered in her eyes.

"I want you to have DNA testing done."

"What!" she asked, almost dropping the glass.

"I want to know one way or the other if that's my baby you're carrying."

"Don't you think that's taking things too far?"

"No, I don't. Tell me the truth, Justine. There isn't another man, is there? Sophie said she didn't know of anyone you were seeing at that time."

"You told Sophie about us?" Justine cried in disbelief.

"Of course not. Lara was just talking to her about the pregnancy and casually asked if she knew who the father was. Sophie said no, that she wasn't aware you were seeing anyone at that time. So why don't you save us both some agony here and tell me the truth. There was no other man in your life in February, was there? That's my baby."

"Why are you being so stubborn about this?" she asked, countering his questions with some of her own. "Why is this so important to you?"

And why was she so dead set against him not knowing the truth? Easy. She didn't want him doing anything for her or the baby out of some sense of duty. She took a sip of the water, more to give herself a little time than because she really wanted it.

"Because to my knowledge, I've never fathered a child before."

There was pain in his eyes. She saw that now. Pain and helplessness and…what? Concern? Truth be told, she'd never seen Wes so…what? Humbled? She knew from past experience and from what she'd heard and read throughout the years that he wasn't usually so tractable. His artistic temperament coupled with his determination to get at the facts—all the facts—made his modus operandi more like that of a steamroller. He must be holding himself back, figuring a composed approach would get him more answers. Answers she wasn't sure she wanted to give him, because somehow she equated the answers he demanded to some sort of commitment.

"What are you saying? That if it is your baby, you want to do the right thing?" she asked.

"Yes."

"Just what is the right thing, in a situation like this? Do you want to pick up the hospital and doctor bills? I have insurance, thanks. Do you want to be my labor coach?" she demanded. When his eyes widened and he paled, she said, "No, I guess not. What is it that you do want then, Wes?"

"I don't know!" he yelled, leaping to his feet. "I do know I'm sick of your games and your double talk. Right now I'd settle for the truth. I'll worry about what to do with it later." His eyes blazed with the anger he'd so far kept under control. "Simple yes or no, Justine. Is that my baby?"

Tired of fighting him, tired of fighting her feelings for him, just tired, she cried, "Yes!"

Maybe, she thought as she saw the truth seep into his consciousness, saw him sink back onto the sofa, just maybe she had finally admitted the truth because she wanted to see what he would do with it.

For long moments he did nothing. Neither of them did. Weary and defeated, Justine pulled out a kitchen chair and sat down, regarding him with a wary expression from across the room.

Finally he turned to look at her, torment in his eyes. "Why didn't you call me when you found out?"

"What was I supposed to say, Wes?" she asked. "It wasn't as if there was anything serious between us. We both know it was spur-of-the-moment, a one-night stand. You have the reputation of being the playboy of Southwest Arkansas. I'm a big girl who knows the score. I'm well aware of the complications of unprotected sex. Was I supposed to come crying to you about the predicament I found myself in? Believe it or not, that isn't my style."

"I do believe it, and it wasn't unprotected sex," he said, latching on to only one part of her explanation.

"Not the first two times, no," she said, shaking her head. "But in the shower…"

A rush of memories swamped her. Exhausted from lovemaking. Sweaty. Sated. Wanting nothing more than to shower and fall asleep. But in the shower, close…so close…touching and kissing, the weariness had vanished beneath another round of hot desire.

"Yeah," Wes said, remembering himself. "The shower."

"So," she said, recapturing the initiative when he didn't say anything else. "Now that you know, what do you plan to do?"

"I don't know." Even though he'd come wanting to know, now that he did, he felt sucker punched. His voice sounded the way he felt. "I've got to get used to all this before I can make any life-altering decisions."

"Heavens, I wouldn't want this to cramp your lifestyle," she said, the sarcasm back in full force.

"Cut me some slack, Justine," he said, weary of her unrelenting attack. "I'm not exactly the Don Juan of Lewiston."

"That's not what I hear."

He ignored the comment. "I'll be glad to help financially."

"The standard remedy of the wealthy. Offer money," Justine said. "But I'm not too proud to take it. By all means, Wes, start him a college fund."

"Him?" The thought that the baby was a boy filled him with a sudden, unexpected euphoria. "It's a boy?"

"I don't know," Justine said, her anger on hold for the moment. "Somehow, I think so, but I don't have anything to back up the feeling."

Wes plowed a hand through his dark hair while thoughts and ideas and concerns whirled through his mind. "This is really insane. I mean, it's...so unexpected."

"No kidding," she agreed dryly.

"I know this must have caused you a lot of problems with your career."

"Some," she said with a shrug. "Nothing I can't handle."

"I'm sorry for that."

"It's only a baby. Not the end of the world, or of my career. Actually it's sort of helped me get things into perspective.

"How's that?"

She took a deep breath and met the question in his eyes squarely. "When I left here, I made myself a vow that I was going to make something of myself. No one would ever look down on me again, and they'd never make fun of me because I was poor or dressed in home-made clothes. I was never going to hate myself for who I was anymore."

"That's why you left? Because you didn't think you measure up?"

"It's one of the reasons."

"Who was doing the measuring, Justine?" he asked. "Who held the measuring standard?"

"The self-righteous of this town," she answered without missing a beat. "Don't act as if it's impossible or that I was imagining things. You were from the bunch that did the measuring."

"Me!" His shock was genuine, but he knew he had to let her talk.

"Do you think I'm stupid, Wes? I know why you

asked me out. You heard I was easy to get into the sack.''

"You're right," he said, knowing it was time for the truth. "That's why I asked you out the first time, but not why I kept asking you out."

She smiled, a bitter twist of her lips. "No, it was the fact that I *was* easy that made you keep coming back for more."

"I won't deny that the sex was part of the reason I kept asking you out, but there was more. I was used to being judged, too, Justine."

"You!"

"Not by the town, but by my dad—remember? We talked about it. I never measured up, never did anything to please him. Like you, I always felt as if I came up short. Until I met you. You made me feel as if I could do or be anything I wanted. You told me to go ahead and become a lawyer to satisfy my dad. But you're the reason I stuck with the painting. You told me to hold on to whatever it was that made me who I really was."

Wes wondered if he was imagining the sudden sheen of tears he saw in her eyes. Suddenly, he, who was considered ruthless, cold and calculating, felt near tears himself.

"That's why I'm holding on to this baby," she said, her voice quavering with emotion. "Because no matter how sophisticated I told myself I'd become through the years, it just isn't me to get rid of it, even though I was encouraged to do just that."

Wes's breath caught in his throat, and his heart missed a beat. He'd never entertained the thought that she'd considered abortion. Feeling as if he were drowning in a sea of feeling, he grasped the one thing she'd mentioned that she hadn't explained. "How did the baby help you put things into perspective?"

"It helped me see that relationships and people are far more important than things or success."

"It's funny that you're just now figuring that out," Wes said, a ghost of a smile playing around his finely shaped lips. "You taught me that years ago."

He saw the surprise in Justine's eyes before she gave a little cry and her hands moved to her stomach.

"Are you okay? he asked, coming up out of his seat.

"I'm fine," she said with a little smile. "But he's very athletic some days, and sometimes he kicks really hard."

Wes crammed his hands into his pockets. "You can actually feel it?" he asked, knowing intellectually that she could, but unable to get his mind to fathom the whole process. Except for his niece Belle, babies and children hadn't been a part of his life, and he didn't recall Lara commenting on her pregnancy—good or bad.

Justine smiled, a smile that made her whole face light up like a kid who realized Santa had fulfilled each and every wish on Christmas morning. "Yeah. It's great. Do you want to feel?"

As soon as she said the words, Wes could see that she wanted to take them back. As intimate as they had been, and it didn't get any more intimate than the night they'd spent together in Chicago, this was an invitation to intimacy of a different sort. This request opened the door for a whole new arena, something the uneasiness in Justine's eyes told him she was unsure of.

"You don't mind?" he asked, as startled by the offer as she seemed to be.

"No," she said, but then, how could she object after making the offer?

Suddenly he wanted to put his hands on her and feel his baby moving. *His baby.* The thought was at once exhilarating and frightening. A baby that he and Justine had created in—what? Love? He thought, moving closer to her. Though he wasn't ready to call his feelings for Justine love, his gut—the same gut that guided him on his hardest cases—told him as it had the night in Chicago, that the feeling was closer to love than lust and always had been.

Her eyes never left him. He was as drawn to them as he was to the sight of her sitting in the kitchen chair, the lapels of her robe gaping and exposing the gentle swell of a creamy, blue-veined breast above the scooped neckline of her gown. A breast much fuller than he remembered.

As he neared her, she had to tip back her head, her gaze clinging to his as if she were watching to see if he planned to make any sudden moves. Her lips were parted, their soft fullness an invitation he found hard to refuse. Neither spoke. Pregnancy became her. There was something sexy about it, he thought, even though a part of his brain chastised him for thinking such a thing.

Wes stopped in front of her. Uncertain how best to proceed, he dropped to his knees and heard Justine suck in a little breath. Their eyes were almost at a level; her knees nearly brushed his chest. Her tongue darted out, leaving a sheen of moisture on their ripe fullness. Everything about her was ripe—her mouth, so full and bee-stung, her breasts, heavy and lush beneath the satin of her gown, and her belly, swollen with his child.

Desire flared in him, hot and heady. He wanted to

kiss her, to taste the soft fullness of her flesh, to fill his hands with her. But just as urgent was the sudden need to paint her. In this gown and robe, her hair a curly tangle over her shoulders, one breast partly exposed, the heat of a blush blooming on her cheeks and her body ripe and fruitful. He wanted to put it all on canvas, so that if he ever forgot the way she looked, he could take out the portrait and remember. So that one day he could say to his son or daughter, ''This was your mother when she was carrying you. Do you see how beautiful she was?''

Unable to help himself, he reached out, turning his hand to brush the crest of her cheekbone with his knuckles. Justine's eyes drifted shut for a second, then opened. She gave a little shake of her head and, before his fingers did more than graze her skin, she caught his wrist with one hand.

Disappointment surged through him, even though he knew she was right. Kissing her, doing anything physical would only further complicate an already complicated situation. Still, he ached to taste her.

You're on dangerous ground, Grayson. The part of him that wasn't drowning in a sea of sensation tried to make him see reason. He struggled to calm the tumult inside him. ''What do I do?''

Almost self-consciously, she parted her legs so he could move closer. He did. Memories swirled around him, and from the hot color that bloomed on her cheeks, he knew she remembered, too. She pressed her lips together in a determined line, as if by doing so she could gain control of her thoughts and the moment.

''Put your hand here.'' She took the hand she held and placed in on the swell of her stomach, then reached for his other hand.

He was surprised at how full and hard she felt. Not so surprised at how full and hard he felt. Get a grip. "What now?"

"Just wait."

He waited. Nothing.

"Sometimes it takes a while."

He nodded, senses snared by the scent of her perfume, something light and floral that made him think of magnolias in the moonlight…and about Justine's legs wrapped around him, her body moving in perfect synchronization with his. Flesh fused by a film of perspiration. Hearts hammering out a pagan rhythm.

A sudden, sharp thump beneath his palm scattered his erotic thoughts like chafe in a strong wind. Then the bulge seemed to roll and dip, like flag rippling in a stiff breeze, snatching Wes's breath and making him feel weak all over.

"Did you feel that?" he asked, his gaze flying to Justine's.

"How could I not?"

He frowned. "Does it hurt?"

"It doesn't actually hurt," she said with a shake of her head. "Not really. But it can get uncomfortable, if he's doing jumping jacks or backflips."

The baby moved again, creating a hard knot. Wes couldn't suppress a smile. "This is awesome," he said. "Fantastic."

Acting on impulse, he lowered his ear to her stomach, as if he hoped to hear something. "Can you hear his heartbeat?" he asked, raising his head to look at her.

"Yes," she told him. "With a special wand."

Struggling with a plethora of emotions and a feeling that he might cry, something he hadn't done since he was ten years old, Wes didn't say anything for a moment. When he was able to speak, the words came out in a husky rasp. "Thank you."

Justine's eyebrows drew together in a frown. "For what?"

For not having an abortion.

He couldn't force himself to say the words. Even thinking them brought a sharp pain to his heart. "For not taking the easy way out."

Chapter Six

On Monday Justine woke to the sound of Donovan's truck as it pulled down the lane to the greenhouses. To her surprise, she'd slept like a baby. Almost immediately after thanking her, Wes told her he would see her after the funeral and left. She could tell he was still in a bit of shock to learn he was the father of her baby, and she knew he'd been affected by the first-time experience of feeling the baby's movements.

She'd expected to lie awake worrying about his next move but instead had fallen asleep almost as soon as her head hit the pillow. She supposed that telling Wes the truth had eased the strain she'd been under for so long and allowed her to get some much-needed rest. But it was morning already, the morning of her mother's funeral, which would be held at the small non-denominational church Opal had attended after Gene abandoned her and Molly and the boys.

The funeral was to be held at ten, and from experience, Justine knew they could count on people coming by the house to eat until at least one. Molly could only stay until Tuesday evening, so they had to start cleaning out their mother's things as soon as everyone left. And they would have to stay with it until they were finished. Sophie had volunteered to help, which would make things easier.

Opal left a living will, giving the house to Molly, which was fine with Justine, who would never be able to bring herself to stay there. Other than her personal items, Opal hadn't owned much of value—two or three good antique pieces of some glassware and dishes that were pretty if not truly collectible. Justine and Molly would divvy the things up, and once they and Sophie had taken a few personal mementos, Justine would call the auction house and Goodwill to pick up the rest. When that was done, there would be no reason for her to stay, and she'd head back to Nashville to await the birth of her baby and Wes's decision, whatever that might be.

A few days ago she hadn't wanted to come back to Lewiston. She would rather—as her mama used to say—have had a root canal. But now that she was back, around family, around people who cared for her, Justine realized it wasn't the place itself that she'd convinced herself she hated, just the situation she'd found herself in and a few of the town's inhabitants.

Like all small towns, there was more than a fair share of gossip and meddling in things that ought to be left alone. There was a certain amount of bigotry and an element of snobbery. But there was something nice about driving down the street without encountering any traffic jams, something comforting about having people recognize you and wave. Something reassuring about knowing the grocer, the pharmacist, the mortician. It was a pleasurable experience being a person to the doctor, not just a number on an insurance form.

On the whole, the people were good, hardworking people, who rallied round in times of trouble, who might talk about you over the dinner table, but then bring you a casserole when you were sick. Maybe they gossiped because there wasn't much else to do for entertainment, Justine reasoned.

As she'd told Wes, the pregnancy had given her a new perspective. Coming back to Lewiston had only reinforced the decision she'd made before coming. As exciting as her brief, blossoming singing career had been, the breakup with her manager, Pete Bennett, who'd wanted her to get rid of the baby because it would be a hindrance to her upward climb, had been a real eye-opener. Even though she knew it was possible to have both a family and a career, she knew it took its toll.

Traveling from town to town for concerts was wearying for an adult. Dragging a child along would be a nightmare. Besides, it wasn't fair to the child to be cooped up in a moving bus all day. The alternative was to leave the baby behind with a competent caretaker, which had the advantage of the child living in a stable environment, of being around familiar things, people and places. The only thing he wouldn't have was his mother.

Justine imagined coming home from a road trip, going to her baby and having it turn from her to the more familiar nanny. It wasn't a thought that appealed.

She'd decided that the singing would have to go—at least for now. There were several singers who'd made the choice of raising babies over careers, and even though some of those careers had never taken off again, she doubted if any of those women regretted the choice they'd made. Besides, she'd made a good living at writing songs for years before she'd recorded anything, and she was good at it. Even now, singers whose careers had skyrocketed with a Justine Sutton song still called her routinely looking for new material. It was gratifying to know her song-writing skills were still in demand.

All things considered, coming back to her childhood home hadn't been the ordeal she expected, even though she had been forced to face Wes. Under different circumstances, she might even enjoy living here. In fact, she thought, making a sudden decision, when she got back to Nashville, she would start looking for a little town within driving distance of the city, some place where she could bring up the baby in a small-town atmosphere, a place where she would know his teachers and the parents of his friends and his baseball coaches.

But first, there was the funeral.

The September morning was already warm when the car arrived to pick up Justine and take her to the church. She, Molly, Donovan, Lara, Sophie, Reed and Cassidy were the only ones seated on the front pew, which had been set aside for Opal Malone's family members. She especially appreciated Reed's presence. He had to fly to St. Louis to take a deposition for an upcoming custody case as soon as the service was over, and his coming was going to make his catching his flight chancy.

With her back to the other mourners, Justine had no idea how many people had actually come to the service, but Sophie, who sneaked a peek just before it began, said it was a good crowd.

The preacher, a middle-age man Justine had never met before this weekend, stood before the mourners and gave them the pertinent facts about Opal's life. Justine, whose mind was filled with memories, tuned most of it out, as she did the sermon, which was blessedly short. In less than thirty minutes they were whisked out the side door to the limo, which would follow the hearse to the cemetery, some five miles out in the country. Opal would be laid to rest next to Justine's father, with Ruby, her beloved twin, two headstones away.

Though funerals weren't on Wes's list of favorite things to do, he attended Opal Malone's with his aunt and his niece. Reed sat with Sophie in the family pew, and Lara was next to Donovan. None of them felt it was necessary for Belle to be there, so she sat with Wes and Isabelle.

Wes noted that Arnold and Mildred Grimes were among those who'd come to pay their last respects, as was Frank Fontaine, owner of the local grocery store and his wife. Even Rowland Hardisty made an appearance, though he seemed to be alone and made no attempt to speak to her or the others. Reed's mother was nowhere to be seen. Wes found his attention was less on the sermon than on Justine, who sat with her back to him.

He'd spent a sleepless night, coming to grips with the news about the baby and trying to decide exactly what he was going to do about it. He still wasn't sure what the best course of action might be.

At the cemetery another song was sung, another brief message of departure was spoken, and the final prayer was said. Wes stood back and watched the line form for those who wished to speak their last words of regret, support and hope to the family. While Isabelle offered her condolences, Belle stood next to Wes looking sad, while Wes, his hands in his pockets, regarded Justine's profile.

Finally people began drifting to their cars. Isabelle lingered, talking to Sophie and Reed. Justine was standing near the chair she'd just vacated, waiting for the director to usher them back to the limo, when Wes went over to her.

"We need to talk."

Justine dabbed at the corners of her eyes and nodded.

"I'll come by the house later," he told her.

"We're having lunch at Donovan's, and then we're going to Mama's to start going through her things."

"I'll find you."

In a gesture that surprised her, he reached out and placed a gentle hand on her abdomen. "How's my boy this morning?"

"Fine," she replied in a reedy voice.

His hand moved lower, to the underside of her belly. A soft breath hissed from her lips. He liked knowing his touch affected her. "Is he doing calisthenics this morning?"

"No. He's been pretty quiet." Justine clutched at the aluminum pole that held the mortuary's shade tent in place and glanced around to see if anyone was watching. "Wes. Someone might see."

Feeling reckless, he offered her a hint of a smile and said, "So? Did you think you could keep his paternity a secret forever?"

"I planned to give it a good try," she said, glaring at him with tear-dampened eyes.

His smile broadened. "We'll talk," he said again, then turned and left her standing there.

"Miss Sutton?"

Justine turned. "Yes?"

"The car is ready to take you home now."

From the vantage point of Wes's front seat, Isabelle watched the exchange between her nephew and Justine Sutton. Very interesting, she thought. Very interesting. And meaningful. She did a little quick calculating and realized that Justine had gotten pregnant at approximately the same time Wes had been in Chicago. She saw him put his hand on Justine's stomach. Hmm. Very interesting. And certainly within the realm of possibility.

Isabelle watched the funeral director approach them, then say something to Justine. She watched Justine turn and walk toward the group gathered near the limo where Reed and Donovan stood talking, while Molly, Lara and Cassidy stood nearby. As Isabelle watched, Lara said something to Molly who turned to answer. Isabelle felt as if the world shifted on its axis. She'd known Molly Malone since birth, but until the day before, she hadn't really seen the child in years. No, not a child. Molly was a woman, and the feeling that she reminded Isabelle of someone had taunted her ever since she'd taken the food to Donovan's. Now she knew exactly who that someone was.

Lara.

The similarity wasn't superficial. It was more than dark hair in a like haircut. More than tall slenderness. It was in the shape of their eyebrows, the curve of their cheeks, the straight, patrician nose that Lara had inherited from her father.

What are you thinking, Isabelle? That Lara and

*Molly Malone look alike because they have the same
father? Preposterous!*

But was it? Really? Phil had certainly been a player
after Pamela died, if not before. Isabelle had often
thought it was a blessing that he hadn't remarried, since
his appetites seemed insatiable.

But Phil and Opal Malone? Opal had had a husband,
but then, matrimony had never been much of a deter-
rent, and Gene Malone hadn't been much of a prize.
Opal had been a knockout when she was young, and
Phil *had* deeded her that house upon his death. Maybe
it wasn't so far-fetched after all.

Isabelle wasn't the kind to go off half-cocked. The
matter would take some looking into before she was
ready to acknowledge it as truth and think about what—
if anything—might need to be done about it.

Justine shoved her sunglasses onto her nose and followed the funeral director to the car where the rest of
her family waited. She glanced to her right and saw
Rowland Hardisty getting into his car. From behind the
safety of her sunglasses, she saw his gaze move from
her to the place where she knew Wes was still standing.
The look on Rowland's face was one of thoughtful consideration.

Justine gave an involuntary shiver and slipped into
the back seat.

Rowland had only attended Opal Malone's funeral
because it was expected of him, but maybe it was a
good thing he had. Coming had shed some light on a
situation that had intrigued him since Friday; namely
who was the father of Justine Sutton's baby? As a disturbing image of Wes Grayson and Justine standing to-

gether flashed through his mind, Rowland figured he'd stumbled onto the answer to that question quite by accident.

A man didn't just go around putting his hands on a pregnant woman's abdomen, not even a man as aggressive as Wes, unless there was more between them. Wes was the epitome of the Southern gentleman, and he would never do anything so overtly intimate in public. Yet Wes—obviously believing he was unobserved— had touched Justine, and she had allowed it. There had been a smile on his lips and a softness in Justine's features that screamed of intimacy. Interesting. Rowland wondered how it had happened. When? He wasn't even aware that the two knew each other, except in passing.

What he did know was that Phil Grayson would turn over in his grave if he thought his son was involved with a woman like Justine. She'd always been loose, but no doubt the lifestyle she lived in Nashville lent itself to all sorts of scandalous doings. There were bound to have been men in the years since she'd left— lots of men. How could there not be? She was a hot woman if Rowland had ever seen one—from the red hair to the lush curves that she showed off to best advantage on her music videos.

No, Phil would not be pleased that his only son had taken up with a woman like Justine, more specifically, Justine herself. Rowland knew how it felt to have a child marry beneath his station. Despite his lies and machinations, Reed had just married Sophie Delaney, the little slut he'd gotten pregnant years ago. And Lara, Rowland's former daughter-in-law, had married Sophie's brother, Donovan. Now Rowland's precious Belle had an ex-convict for a stepfather.

Rowland shook his head. What was the world coming

to? And why didn't Reed and Lara have any more sense than to take up with people far below them on the social ladder? They claimed love, but love was just a word that made sex more palatable to people with consciences.

Whistling tunelessly through his teeth, Rowland considered the situation and asked himself what he should do. He and Phil had been as close as two friends could be, sharing drinks, talking about business and swapping tales of their conquests. Of course it had been different for Phil. He'd been a widower. Rowland, on the other hand, was just the kind of man who'd never let little things like vows, rings and a piece of paper stop him from sleeping with whomever he wanted. Rowland stopped whistling. Maybe there was something he could do. He hadn't been able to persuade his family members that they were making a mistake, but maybe he could give Wes a talking to.

Rowland closed his eyes, pleased by the brilliance of his plan. It never occurred to him to gauge himself by the same standard he used to judge the morality of others. And if it had, he'd have dismissed it. He was a law unto himself. He made his own rules and lived his life the way he wanted.

Everyone had cleared out of Donovan's house by one-thirty, except some ladies from the church who insisted on staying until everything was cleaned up. They also insisted that Justine, Molly and Sophie go ahead and start the task of sorting through their mother's things, so the three women loaded into Sophie's car and drove the seven miles to the Malone house, which was just outside the city limits on the other side of town.

The place looked nice, Justine thought, as Molly

pulled into the driveway. The taupe-hued frame house with the burgundy shutters had been painted recently. The shrubs along the front were trimmed, and the flower beds were weed free, even though the drooping flower heads spoke of their weary struggle with the lingering heat of summer.

Sophie pulled the car to a stop, and the trio got out and went up onto the porch. Molly unlocked the door and pushed it open. Justine followed her inside, her heart beating heavily. She walked into the living room, noting the changes and waiting for the memories to fill her, but there was nothing in the house to remind her of the past, except a few pictures and the occasional chair or knickknack. The dark paneling and antiquated lighting were gone. Opal had painted and papered and covered the battered hardwood floors with plush carpet. The kitchen was bright and cheery, with a border of teacups circling the ceiling and a collection of teapots and cups scattered on various shelves around the room. Copper pots hung from a rack over the island that housed the stove top, and green plants sat in the sunny west window.

"It's so nice!" Justine said, standing in the middle of the room and turning in a circle. "It doesn't look anything like it did when I was at home."

"It's been a long time," Sophie said. "Mama told me that once Gene left, Aunt Opal wanted to get rid of everything that reminded her of him. Sorry, Molly," she added, casting an apologetic glance at the younger woman. As sorry a person as he'd been and no doubt still was, Gene Malone was still Molly's father.

"It's okay." Molly tried to smile. "Where should we start?"

"Why not the kitchen?" Sophie suggested.

They decided to donate all the cooking utensils to Goodwill, the canned and boxed food to the church for distribution to the needy, and perishable food and freezer stuff to the neighbors. Molly wanted the copper pans, Sophie wanted the teapots and knew Donovan would like to have the cookie jar they found stuck in the pantry that she remembered sitting on their aunt's cabinet when they were kids. Justine took the mismatched dishes. She'd always liked the way none of them matched but seemed to look pretty on the table just the same. They'd go with her own collection nicely. The green plants would go to the nursing home.

They moved to the bedroom and after a quick look decided that there were no clothes they wanted to keep. They did find four brand-new quilts. The tops were pieced on a sewing machine, but quilted by hand, each tiny stitch as precise as if it had been measured. As they looked at each other with tear-filled eyes, Sophie said, "She must have worked on these right to the end."

"There's a name pinned to the top of each one," Molly said. "One for Donovan, Sophie, me and you, Justine, even though you never came to see her."

Justine heard Sophie's gasp of surprise even as her gaze met her sister's. A subtle accusation resided in Molly's dark eyes, and something akin to a challenge. Though they had been careful to maintain civility the past couple of days, Justine had, from time to time, sensed the anger that simmered beneath her sister's calm demeanor. She'd known they would come to some sort of showdown before they went their separate ways, but knowing it was coming hadn't made her ready for it.

Suddenly weary, and overcome with a piercing sense of sorrow unlike anything she'd experienced since she'd arrived, Justine sank onto the edge of the bed, something they were never allowed to do as children, because it would break down the edge of the mattress. She looked to Sophie for encouragement, but her cousin's only reply was a nod that seemed to say without words that this confrontation was a good thing, something that needed to happen, *had* to happen, should have happened long ago.

"When I was little, it hurt," Molly said, pressing a hand to her heart. Her eyes filled with tears. "Mama would cry whenever she did talk to you on the phone, and I'd cry with her. The few times we went to see you, she was depressed for weeks when we got back. As I grew older, I became angry with you because you hardly ever called and never came home."

"And now?" Justine prompted softly.

Molly met Justine's questioning gaze with an enviable directness. "Now? I'm old enough to realize that something happened, that there was some reason you separated yourself from us...from her, but I swear, I can't imagine what it might be. From where I stand, all I can see is that she was so proud of you, and you couldn't have cared less about her."

The bluntness of Molly's statement was like a physical blow that actually caused Justine to flinch. Sophie stood in the corner of the room, watching and listening.

"So you could say I stayed angry with you most of the time for the way you ignored her, but you sent me a check every month, and I cashed it because it made my life easier, which makes me a hypocrite, I guess. At least you aren't that."

Justine let her sister's comments sink into her mind and her soul. "Thanks for your honesty," she said finally. "But the part about my not caring isn't true."

''Then what is, Justine?'' Molly asked in a soft voice. ''Whatever it is that's festering inside you, why don't you tell me, so I'll understand? Then maybe we can both get past it and move on.''

There it was again. A variation on the theme of the same song Sophie and Donovan had been singing. Justine bowed to the inevitable. There was no escaping the showdown. She'd postponed it long enough as it was. She wondered how she could tell Molly what a lowlife her father was without widening the gap that already existed between the two of them. Maybe there was no way, but maybe Molly deserved to know the truth, anyway.

She glanced at Sophie, who nodded her encouragement. ''It isn't pretty,'' Justine said, offering Molly and herself a way out.

Molly shrugged.

''It involves Gene.''

Molly grew pale, and her eyes darkened with anger. ''I was only five years old when Dad walked out on me and Mom and the boys, but I remember enough to know he wasn't a nice person. You don't have to worry about sullying my fond memories of him, because there aren't any.''

How much had Molly seen as a child? How much did she already suspect? Justine wondered. She took a deep breath and blurted. ''Gene turned me out, and Mama let him.''

''What?'' the expression on Molly's face was one of stunned disbelief, a shock that echoed in Sophie's mournful cry.

''It was right after you were born,'' Justine said, keeping her gaze focused on the four-poster bed. ''Mama had a hard time with you, and she couldn't seem to get her strength back. Money was tight, as usual." She glanced at Molly. "You knew Gene had a gambling problem?"

"Mama told me, later," Molly said.

"Well, we were way behind on the rent and everything else for that matter. One night Gene told me to get fixed up and take a month's rent to Mr. Grayson out at his place on the lake.

"I remember this horrified look on Mama's face. 'No, Gene!' she said, but he told her to shut her mouth or he'd shut it for her."

Caught up in remembrances, Justine's eyes had taken on a faraway look.

"They went outside, and I heard them arguing." The statement was accompanied by a look of surprise, as if Justine had just remembered that bit of the story. "Then they came back inside. Mama looked relieved, and Gene was yelling 'Fine! Fine! Let him put us out on the street, then.' He asked her what about the letter they'd gotten that said all the back rent had to be paid or we'd be evicted in thirty days. Mama told him it would be okay, that Mr. Grayson wouldn't kick us out. Not now.

"A couple of days later, she went over to Aunt Ruby's. Your daddy had been on a rampage," Justine said to Sophie, "and your Mama was in pretty bad shape." she drew a deep breath and let it out slowly. "I was doing my homework, when Gene told me to go get fixed up. He had an errand for me to run."

Go get a bath. And use some of those new bath salts I got your mama for Christmas.

The memory of the words was as clear as if Gene was just now saying them. Trapped in the past, Justine repeated them in a voice totally devoid of emotion.

Wary, Justine had done as she was told. When she came out of the bathroom, she saw that Gene had laid her mother's red party dress on the bed.

"Put on that dress and fix yourself up really pretty, Jussie. You want to make a good impression."

"Who am I trying to impress?"

"Phil Grayson. Now step on it."

Justine had always loved the dress, a low-cut red satin with a short flounced skirt. Thrilled that she was being allowed to wear it, she piled her hair up on top of her head in a riot of curls and applied makeup that added at least five years to her age. When she finished, a stranger stared back at her from the mirror. The red satin clung to her body as if she'd been melted and poured into it. The bodice dipped low, revealing far too much of her breasts. She didn't look anything like herself.

As she stared at herself in the spotty mirror, she realized that she didn't look glamorous the way she'd imagined she would. Something had gone wrong. Instead of the class she'd hoped to gain by wearing the dress, she looked like some fancy floozie, or a cheap barfly.

"Hurry up, will you?" Gene bellowed from the other room. "We can't keep him waiting all night."

Him. Mr. Grayson. She was taking the rent. The wariness she'd experienced the night of her mother's outburst returned. Her stomach began to churn sickeningly, but she found herself opening the bedroom door.

"Turn around and let me get a good look at you," Gene said.

He instructed Justine to do a little pirouette and whistled in appreciation. "Now don't you look nice," he

PLAY SILHOUETTE'S

LUCKY HEARTS
GAME

AND YOU GET

FREE BOOKS!
A FREE GIFT!
YOURS TO KEEP!

TURN THE PAGE AND DEAL YOURSELF IN...

Play **LUCKY HEARTS** for this...

*exciting **FREE** gift!*
**This surprise mystery gift
could be yours free**

when you play **LUCKY HEARTS!**
**...then continue your lucky streak
with a sweetheart of a deal!**

1. Play Lucky Hearts as instructed on the opposite page.

2. Send back this card and you'll receive 2 brand-new Silhouette Special Edition® novels. These books have a cover price of $4.50 each in the U.S. and $5.25 each in Canada, but they are yours to keep absolutely free.

3. There's no catch! You're under no obligation to buy anything. We charge nothing— ZERO—for your first shipment. And you don't have to make any minimum number of purchases—not even one!

4. The fact is thousands of readers enjoy receiving their books by mail from the Silhouette Reader Service™. They enjoy the convenience of home delivery...they like getting the best new novels at discount prices, BEFORE they're available in stores...and they love their *Heart to Heart* subscriber newsletter featuring author news, horoscopes, recipes, book reviews and much more!

5. We hope that after receiving your free books you'll want to remain a subscriber. But the choice is yours—to continue or cancel, any time at all! So why not take us up on our invitation, with no risk of any kind. You'll be glad you did!

Visit us online at

www.eHarlequin.com

The Silhouette Reader Service™—Here's how it works:

Accepting your 2 free books and gift places you under no obligation to buy anything. You may keep the books and gift and return the shipping statement marked "cancel." If you do not cancel, about a month later we'll send you 6 additional novels and bill you just $3.80 each in the U.S., or $4.21 each in Canada, plus 25¢ shipping & handling per book and applicable taxes if any.* That's the complete price and — compared to cover prices of $4.50 each in the U.S. and $5.25 each in Canada — it's quite a bargain! You may cancel at any time, but if you choose to continue, every month we'll send you 6 more books, which you may either purchase at the discount price or return to us and cancel your subscription.

*Terms and prices subject to change without notice. Sales tax applicable in N.Y. Canadian residents will be charged applicabl provincial taxes and GST.

If offer card is missing write to: Silhouette Reader Service, 3010 Walden Ave., P.O. Box 1867, Buffalo, NY 14240-1867

SILHOUETTE READER SERVICE
3010 WALDEN AVE
PO BOX 1867
BUFFALO NY 14240-9952

POSTAGE WILL BE PAID BY ADDRESSEE

BUSINESS REPLY MAIL
FIRST-CLASS MAIL   PERMIT NO. 717   BUFFALO, NY

NO POSTAGE
NECESSARY
IF MAILED
IN THE
UNITED STATES

said, his hot gaze roaming over her from head to toe. ''Real nice.''

Justine heard the husky note in his voice that she recognized as the one he used with her mother shortly before they retired to the bedroom.

''I wouldn't mind being in old Phil's place myself.''

Justine's heart stopped for a single beat, and her stomach clenched. The look in his eyes and his comment deepened her suspicion of what was expected of her. Panic rose up inside her on a dark wave of despair.

''Now don't look so upset about it. Phil Grayson is a nice man. If you don't believe me, ask your mama. This is no big deal. Just take him the rent, and if he wants you to stay awhile, it's only because he's a lonely widower who likes company sometimes.'' Gene's tone was his most placating. ''There's nothing to be afraid of. Just be nice and keep him company for a while, and he'll treat you right.''

It sounded reasonable, she thought. *Just…keep him company….* Maybe she was mistaken in what she thought Gene expected of her. Still, as nice as he might be, Phil Grayson was rich and powerful, and he was the father of the boy Justine had had a crush on for the past year.

''Come on,'' he said. ''The big man's waiting.''

Not knowing how to stop things, pushing thoughts of Wes from her mind, Justine followed her stepfather out to his pickup. He didn't say anything to her on the drive to Crescent Lake, but when he dropped her off at the end of the lane and said, ''Your mama and the kids are counting on you, girl. Don't let them down.'' Then he peeled out with a grinding of gears and a cloud of dust.

Counting on her? The fears Gene had allayed came rushing back in force. Her suspicions of what was expected of her deepened along with her panic. With tears in her eyes, Justine stood staring after the vehicle for long moments, wondering how anyone could be so cold and uncaring as Gene and how he could expect her to do what he obviously did. Maybe she would just take the money Gene was sending to Phil Grayson and leave town.

How? On foot? And how far do you think $175 will get you, huh, Justine?

And what about her mother and the baby? And the boys? Her intellect told her it wasn't her place to provide shelter for any of them, but she knew how tough times were and how hard her mother worked to try to make ends meet on the piddling amount of money Gene allowed her for her "household expenses."

Household expenses. Everything came out of that money—from food and utilities to clothes and the extras it took for the baby and school. Justine hadn't even asked for a yearbook, even though she'd worked on the staff and been responsible for several of the layouts. She'd known there was no way her mother could make the money stretch any further, and she hadn't wanted her to fret about it.

Gene made good money as a truck driver. If it weren't for his gambling, there would be plenty of money. He sure didn't do without the way the rest of them did. It wasn't fair, but as her mother would say, that's just the way it is.

Stop being so selfish, Justine. There's more than just yourself to think about. As sorry as Gene was, the rest of her family didn't deserve being kicked out on the street because of his addiction to gambling. Justine thought of the weariness on her mother's face, a face that looked years older since Molly's birth two months

before. Her mom hadn't been able to breastfeed Molly.
For some reason her milk had never come in and they
had had to buy formula, which was expensive.

Cold futility seeped into Justine's soul and settled
next to a growing hatred for her stepfather. There was
nothing to do but meet Mr. Grayson and see what happened. She tried to imagine what was in store for her
but couldn't. All she could think of was Gene and the
look on his face when he'd said he wished he were Phil
Grayson. And the more she thought of Gene, the harder
and colder her heart became. She reasoned that if a body
got cold enough, it couldn't feel. And not feeling had
been the only way she'd known to get through the next
few hours.

"So I went," she told Molly and Sophie. "When I
knocked on the door, Mr. Grayson opened it. He was a
nice-looking man, probably forty, and he resembled
Wes, only older. I told him I had the rent money, and
he just stood there, looking me over from head to toe.
There was this look in his eyes, sort of a—a sadness,
almost. Or maybe it was loneliness, like Gene said.

"Mr. Grayson smiled and told me I looked just like
Mama. He asked me if I was hungry, and I said no,
even though I was. Then he asked me if I wanted something to drink. He was drinking wine, so I said I'd take
some of it. He gave it to me. He told me to go see
which tapes I wanted to listen to. He had a lot popular
stuff, probably Lara's and—and Wes's."

Justine's voice broke on the name, and she lifted her
chin in a gesture of defiance, even though tears ran un-
checked down her cheeks. She wasn't aware she was
crying until she licked her lips and tasted the saltiness
of the tears that had gathered at the corners of her
mouth.

"You don't have to tell me any more," Molly said, her own eyes glistening.

"Yes, I do," Justine said. Now that she'd opened the door to the painful memories, there was no stopping them. And she was glad. Maybe Sophie and Donovan were right. Maybe purging herself of the past was just what she needed.

"We listened to music and I drank the wine and he refilled my glass—I'm not sure how many times—and finally, when I was too tipsy to care, he took me into the bedroom and—" her voice broke on a sob "—and he…we…"

She couldn't finish and wiped at her running nose with the back of her hand. Staring at the hands clenched in her lap, she said, "I guess virgins are worth a lot to a lonely, sad man like Phil Grayson. He let me keep the rent money, and until the day I left, I don't remember hearing Mama and Gene ever talking about the rent being due again."

"So Mama knew?" Molly asked.

Justine nodded. "When Mr. Grayson dropped me off about midnight, Mama was home. She hadn't had to stay with Aunt Ruby after all. Gene was off to God knows where. Mama took one look at me and burst into tears."

"'Why Mama?' I asked her. '"Why do you let him do this to you? Why don't you leave him?' She just shook her head and wiped at her tears and said, 'Where would we go, Justine? What would we do?'

"I told her we could make it. I'd get a job. We could both work. She'd said she was still too weak, and there would be day care for Molly. A woman and two kids couldn't survive on minimum wage." Justine raised her tear-streaked face and looked from Molly to Sophie.

"Then she said a strange thing. She said, 'Better Phil than Gene. Just remember that.'"

Justine shuddered beneath the ugly weight of the memories. "A month or so later, Gene made a move on me while Mama was at the store. At least I was mentally prepared. I fought him off and scratched his cheek real bad. That night I went to Mr. Grayson and asked him for money to leave town. He didn't even ask why, he just went to the safe and got out five hundred dollars cash. I left the next day."

"He didn't ask, because he knew he was guilty. What he did to you was statutory rape," Sophie said. "He probably figured that if you left town, you couldn't cause him any grief." She shook her head. "No wonder he became so altruistic before he died. It also sheds a little more light on why he left this house to Aunt Opal in his will."

Justine offered them a wry smile. "And everyone in town thought he was a good guy."

"You…you think Mama was sleeping with Mr. Grayson?" Molly asked, her eyes opened wide, in more ways than the obvious.

"I do, yes," Justine told her. "And I think Gene knew and condoned it. Looking back, I see that it was the only way she had to keep a roof over our heads while he was off driving the truck. He never cared about her or his boys. He sure as heck didn't care about me."

"So that's the reason you…cut yourself off from Mama," Molly said, understanding dawning.

Justine nodded. "Deep down, I blamed her for not standing up to Gene, for staying in a situation that was so demeaning. And I blamed her for what happened to me, because if she hadn't stayed, it wouldn't have happened."

Justine pushed a swath of hair away from her damp cheek. "She had a point about how hard it would be to make it on her own, especially since she was so sick," she said, as if she were trying to rationalize her mother's actions. "And, in retrospect, I probably didn't have to go through with it. But at the time it seemed like I did." More tears slipped down her cheeks and her gaze found Sophie's, looking for…what? Understanding? Absolution? "I was only sixteen, Sophie."

Sophie lunged away from the wall, where she'd done nothing but listen, and pulled Justine into a close embrace. "Molly, why don't you go make us a pitcher of iced tea?" she suggested.

"Sure," Molly said, disturbed herself by what she'd just heard and understanding that Sophie needed some time alone with Justine to deal with her confession.

Sophie let Justine cry for a while, murmuring, "Let it all out," and smoothing Justine's hair while she cried. Finally, when the worst of the tears had passed, Justine sat back down on the bed. Sophie sat down beside her and took both of Justine's hands in hers.

"What happened wasn't your fault, Justine. You were a victim of Gene's weakness, and Phil Grayson's, too. Even Aunt Opal's. You're right. Maybe if you'd been stronger, less influenced by your mother's situation, you could have refused to do what Gene expected of you. Maybe Aunt Opal should have left Gene. You already know that placing blame doesn't work. The important thing is that you've finally got it out in the open. It's sort of like lancing a boil. You have to get all the bad out before it can heal."

Justine nodded.

"I believe things happen for a reason."

"What possible reason could there be for what Gene asked me to do?"

Sophie offered her a sad smile. "If it hadn't been for the incident with Phil Grayson, you wouldn't have had a way out when Gene made his move on you."

Chapter Seven

Molly made the tea, and they each drank a cup, letting the story that had been told sink in, letting the emotions that had been unleashed ebb. Sophie suggested that maybe they should call it quits and try to finish going through the remnants of Opal's life the next day. Justine insisted that she was fine, that they needed to do all they could because Molly had to leave the following afternoon.

"Are you sure you're up to it?" Sophie asked Justine. "You're still awfully pale."

"You really are, Justine," Molly added. "If we stop for today and don't get finished tomorrow, I trust you to make the best decisions on what to keep and what to save."

"I'm fine," Justine assured them. And I'd never forgive myself if I donated something to someone that you wanted."

"Okay," Sophie said with a nod. "Molly, why don't you drag the stuff out of the bottom of Aunt Opal's bedroom closet and Justine can start going through the cedar chest? I'll start in the spare bedroom."

"Fine," Molly said. "I'd sort of like to have the cedar chest if you don't want it."

"Of course you can have it," Justine said. "And I'd like the bedroom furniture in the spare room, since it was Mama's and Daddy's."

"Okay," Molly said with a nod. They refilled their glasses and carried them to the bedrooms.

"Do you think you can get up if you sit on the floor to go through the cedar chest?" Molly asked.

Justine smiled. "Maybe with a crane."

Molly smiled back and went to the closet across the small room. Justine raised the lid to the chest. Assaulted by the scent of cedar and memories, she lowered herself to the floor. A high school yearbook lay on top. She picked it up and ran her hand over the raised lettering of the vinyl cover. The date was the last year Justine had gone to Lewiston High. It was the yearbook Justine had worked on so hard, the one she'd helped design and lay out. The one there hadn't been enough money to buy.

Somehow, Opal had found the money. Had she clipped more coupons to save more grocery money? Had she taken in ironing? Justine would never know. What she did know was that her mother had understood how important the book was to her. Feeling the threat of tears again, Justine laid the book aside. She'd look at it later, when she wasn't feeling so emotional.

As expected, the contents were a treasure trove of memorabilia, things only a mother would save. Lost baby teeth and locks of hair in yellowing envelopes with names on them, drawings made in elementary school. Ribbons won at track meets. Programs from school plays. School photos. Snapshots of birthdays and holidays. Homemade birthday and Christmas cards covered with crayon and construction paper and glitter.

Justine made stacks for each of them, even Gene's boys. Maybe Molly could get their addresses and send their things to them, not that either of them was the type to care one way or the other. As for herself, she was thrilled. This was the stuff of memories, a chronology and compilation of the tapestry of their lives.

She found a dime store diary beneath a card box filled with snapshots. She frowned. She'd never kept a diary.

"Molly!"

"Yeah?" she said, turning to look at Justine.

"Did you keep a diary?"

"Are you kidding? I hated doing the journals we had to do for English class."

"I just found one," Justine said, drawing it out and opening it. "It's Mama's handwriting."

"Really?" Molly said, getting down from the utility ladder and crossing the room.

"Really." Justine rummaged through the contents of the cedar chest and found three more of the small books. "Hey, Sophie!" she called. "Come on in here."

Sophie came from one of the other bedrooms. "What did you find? Some money hidden away somewhere?"

"I wish," Molly said. "Justine found some diaries of Mama's."

"That's wonderful!" Sophie said. "Diaries can be a good way to find out what really made people tick."

Justine handed one to Molly and one to Sophie. "You look through those. I'll check this one. The one who finishes first can check the last one."

"We really don't have time for this," Molly reminded them.

"I know, but this one dates back to when Mama and my dad were first married," Justine said. "Let's give it thirty minutes or so, then we can get back to work, okay?"

Molly nodded, and they all settled down on the floor and began reading. Justine flipped through her diary, reading a snippet here and there, finding nothing too exciting—how much her mother had loved Hal, how pretty their rent house was. A notation that she was pregnant and so was Ruby. Their babies would be born just weeks apart. Wasn't that neat? And wouldn't it be wonderful if they both had girls? There was a later notation saying she'd named the baby Justine and that Hal was so proud.

Opal was faithful with her entries for days running, then there might not be another entry for months—or even a year or longer. No wonder there were only four diaries in the chest.

"This can't be right," Molly said, the denial causing both Justine and Sophie to look up.

"Find something interesting?" Sophie asked.

Seeing the deathly pallor that had robbed Molly's face of its healthy color, Justine closed her journal. "What is it, Molly?" she asked, her own mind reacting with a burst of concern.

Speechless, Molly handed the book to Justine.

"Whatever it is, read it out loud," Sophie said.

Justine nodded. The entry was dated two days after the date of Molly's birth. In her cramped handwriting, Opal had written about what an ordeal the breech birth had been, how her milk wasn't coming in, and how beautiful Molly was, which made it all worth it.

"'I wonder if Phil has heard the news about his daughter's birth,'" Justine read with growing incredulity.

"His daughter?" Sophie said. "But that sounds as if Molly's dad was Phil Grayson."

"Exactly." Justine kept reading.

"'Surely, he must have. But even if he had, I know he'd never come see us. That would set all Lewiston talking. For all that I believe that basically he's a good man, he is, in many ways a weak man, tormented by indecision and too strongly influenced by what people think, especially Rowland Hardisty.'"

Justine looked at Sophie. "Seems as if good old Rowland was an influence on a lot of people back then."

"Keep reading," Sophie said.

"'Weak?'" Justine read, picking up where she'd left off. "'That's the pot calling the kettle black. What about me? Why don't I stand up to Gene more?'"

Justine glanced at Sophie again. "It must have been something in the genes. Why did Mama stay with him?"

"Lots of reasons," Sophie said. "It was hard for a woman to get along on her own seventeen years ago. Heck, it's hard now. And both our mothers came from the mindset that you took vows and you stuck by them. Don't get me wrong," she hurried to say. "I'm a firm believer in marriage vow and 'until death do us part.' I think that there's too little commitment today, and that people often break up marriages for nothing more than whims. To me that's wrong. A cop-out. On the other hand, I don't think a woman should stay in an abusive situation. And there's more to abuse than being slapped around."

"I don't think either of our mothers had much self-esteem," Molly said. Though her hands were clenched in her lap, and her face was deathly pale, she was holding together remarkably well for someone who'd just found out another man was her father.

"I agree. And when you're told how inadequate you are day after day, you start to believe it. You begin to ask yourself if you could make it on your own, *how* you could make it, if you could find someone else. And when you're convinced you can't, you just stay in a bad situation."

"If he hadn't left us, Mama would probably have stayed with Gene until she died," Molly said.

"Unfortunately, I suspect you're right," Sophie said. "Go on, Justine."

Justine began reading again. "'Maybe Phil and I are better suited than either of us thinks. But whatever happens, he's given me a precious baby girl, and for that I'm thankful. Thankful that if I had to have another baby, it's Phil's, not Gene's.'"

"That's pretty plain," Sophie said. She glanced at Molly. The expression on her face was one of pained disbelief. "Are you okay?"

"Yeah," she said, brushing at the tears she couldn't hold back any longer. "Go on, Justine," she said in a husky voice. "Let's hear it all."

"'I'm writing this so that one day Molly will find it and know the truth about her father, her heritage. The truth is that at my husband's insistence, because he gambles all the money away, I regularly sleep with the landlord in exchange for the rent. An ugly fact of life. No, that isn't exactly true. The first few times were agony, but after a while, I began to look forward to meeting Phil. Going to be with him is like escaping prison and going to a place in the sun. No bill collectors, no worries. He treats me well and is always considerate of my feelings. I don't love him. I haven't truly loved anyone since Hal. It's strictly a financial arrangement, but if it weren't for the time with Phil, I think I might very well go insane.'

"That's all," Justine said. "The passage just ends."

A little sob escaped Molly, and tears spilled down her cheeks. Sophie handed her a tissue from a box on the nightstand. "I always thought she was such a saint," Molly said. "She was always so gentle and kind to people. And she was so patient and nonjudgmental."

"She was all that, Molly," Sophie said in a gentle voice. "But none of us is perfect. Justine and my Cassidy can both tell you how painful it is to find out your parents have feet of clay. We all make mistakes, and we all do things that are wrong. The main thing for you to remember is that despite the circumstances, your mother wanted you and loved you."

Molly nodded.

"Is there anything else we should hear?" Sophie asked.

"The next entry was written a few days after the night Gene sent me to Phil Grayson's cabin," Justine said. The ink had run in places, and the paper was spotted with what could only be her mother's tears.

"I...I don't think I can read it."

Sophie held out her hand, and Justine handed over the journal. "I know this is painful for you both, but it's good to find out. Really." When there was no response, Sophie began to read.

"'She's gone. When I got home, Justine's things were gone. She left me a note saying she couldn't live here anymore because Gene had cornered her in the bathroom. I can't blame her, but dear God! What kind of a monster am I married to? I know the reason is more than Gene making a move on her. She still has hard feelings for what happened last month. I can't believe Gene waited until I was gone and sent Justine to Phil in my place. I despise him for that, and I despise Phil for taking my baby's innocence. Even more, I despise myself for not realizing what the two of them had planned.

"'I should have known what Gene was up to. He always gets what he wants, and he was hellbent on sending Justine to Phil so he wouldn't kick us out. I know for a fact that Justine hates me. It was in her eyes when she got home, and I see it every time she looks at me. She thinks we should leave, but where would we go, and how would I support three of us? I hope—pray—that in time she'll stop blaming me.'"

There was a notation when Phil died and deeded the house to Opal free and clear in what Opal described as his attempt to assuage his guilt. She noted, too, that he'd left another house to a widow across town, probably, she thought, so no one would attach any special significance to his leaving the house to her. God forbid anyone find out that Molly was his child or that he was anything less than what the community perceived him to be.

Sophie closed the journal. Justine looked at her sister. Though Molly had seemed accepting of the reasons behind Justine's actions once she'd learned the truth, maybe this would give her an even greater insight into what it was like to be caught up in something you had little or no control over.

"Well, look on the bright side," Justine said with an attempt at humor.

"Is there a bright side?" Molly asked with a sniff.

"Definitely. Not one drop of Gene Malone's blood flows in your veins. That has to be a bit of a relief."

"Yeah," Molly said, with a slight smile. "You're right. It is."

"What are you going to do now?" Sophie asked.

"About what?"

"Are you going to tell Lara and Wes you're their half sister?"

The very idea appeared to stun Molly. "I am, aren't I?"

"According to Aunt Opal, most definitely."

"I can't believe I didn't see the resemblance to Lara," Justine said. They both had that dark, glossy hair, and the shape of their chins and the way they carried themselves was the same. They both had a pragmatic approach to life, traits they must have inherited from their father.

"Well, you haven't been around the two of them together," Sophie said.

"There's no way I resemble Mrs. Hardisty—I mean Mrs. Delaney," Molly said. "She's gorgeous."

"So are you," Justine told her.

"What do you think Lara and Wes would say if I told them?"

Good question, one Justine had been asking herself. Did they already know? Doubtful. "I'm not sure. Do you want to?"

"I don't know."

"There's a lot at stake here, Molly," Sophie said. "If you can prove Phil's paternity through a blood test, you could probably get part of the money he left Lara and Wes. He amassed quite a lot of money and real estate during his life. It's only a drop in the bucket to what Lara's mother's side of the family has, but your part would be a nice nest egg.''

Molly's eyes gleamed at the prospect of inheriting some money. The glimmer soon faded. ''I'm not sure it would be worth all the trouble I'd stir up.''

''You have a point,'' Justine conceded. ''But Lara and Wes are both fair people, though Wes will make you jump through hoops before he gives an inch.''

''He won't want to part with any of his money, huh?''

''Money has nothing to do with it,'' Sophie told her. ''His personality does.''

''I don't have to decide today, do I?''

''Of course not,'' Justine said, reaching out and patting her sister's hand. ''I think we've all had enough disclosure and trauma for one day.''

Molly turned her hand and captured Justine's fingers in tight grip. ''I'm sorry I judged you so harshly.''

''And I'm sorry I judged Mama so harshly,'' Justine said. ''I think I let my hatred for Gene bleed over into my feelings for her. It seemed like every time we talked on the phone or I saw her, it all came back, uglier than ever. I didn't want to think about it—not ever—so it was just easier to cut her out of my life.''

''She missed you, Justine.''

Justine felt tears gathering in her eyes. ''And I'll miss her for the rest of my life.''

Wes dropped off Belle, then drove home Isabelle, whose driver was still sick. When she asked him to join her for coffee in the garden, which, thanks to an extensive irrigation system was still lush and beautiful even at summer's end, he agreed. For once in his life he was at a point where aggression, intelligence and a keen sense of justice did him no good. His emotions were too involved for him to make any clear-cut decisions for the future. He waffled between what he thought was right, what he thought was the best for all, and what he thought he wanted. Isabelle was a wise woman. Maybe she could shed some light on his dilemma.

They sat at a glass-topped, wrought-iron table in the midst of the herb garden. The scent of chamomile and thyme, crushed beneath their footsteps, wafted on the air, while the chittering of squirrels and hummingbirds vied with the songbirds for attention. A variety of butterflies flitted indiscriminately from the pineapple sage to the monarda, while honeybees buzzed from flower to flower.

"What's on your mind, Weston?" Isabelle asked, after she'd poured their coffee from the silver urn.

Wes stirred a spoonful of sugar into the dark liquid. "What makes you think something's on my mind?"

"Hmm?" Isabelle said, pretending to consider the question. "Perhaps because I know you as well as anyone, and it isn't like you to be so...social, shall we say?"

He smiled. "Meaning I'm antisocial?"

Isabelle poured cream into her cup and reached for the sugar. "Meaning you like your solitude and your own company, which isn't necessarily a bad thing." She smiled. "I've always rather liked my own company, as well. So tell me what's bothering you."

"What do you do if you get yourself into a situation and you aren't certain what to do to get out of it?"

"That depends on what kind of situation it is," Isabelle said, lifting the delicate Haviland cup to her lips.

"I'm at least partly to blame for it."

"Then you should accept your part of the responsibility."

"I know that." Wes rubbed a hand over his cheek, already showing the shadow of a beard. "I'm willing to do that. But what if I want more?"

Isabelle had never liked watching fish flounder at the end of the line. She either wanted them to get off the hook, or she wanted to get them in the boat. She had neither the patience nor the inclination to watch Wes flounder about, when she could end his misery.

"Would this have anything to do with that little scene I saw between you and Justine Sutton at the cemetery?" she asked.

"You saw us talking?"

"What I saw was you touching her in a most intimate way, which tells me at least one thing."

"And what's that?"

"The baby is yours, isn't it, Wes?"

Isabelle had always been sharp, and her advancing years didn't seem to have affected that keen mentality, even though that mental sharpness sometimes cut you to the bone. "Yes."

"Would you like to tell me how it happened?"

Why not? Why should he keep Isabelle in the dark, especially since she carried so much clout? She was a loyal ally and a formidable foe. It would be best to have her on his side, armed with the truth.

He started with the bet when he was in college and how he and Reed had asked out Justine and Sophie. He told his aunt how he'd felt about her and how he'd been devastated when she'd left town without a word. Then he told her about Chicago. "I know it's my baby. She finally admitted it."

Isabelle listened without interrupting. "And you believe her?"

He did. Intellect told him Justine could be involved with someone else, but something—his ego, maybe, or some deep-seated need to believe otherwise—made him trust her. "Yeah," he said. "I do."

"And how do you feel about being a father?"

"Scared," he admitted.

"Being responsible for the nurturing of a child is a frightening prospect," Isabelle said, nodding. "But you're up to the task."

"Do you really think so?"

"Of course I do. You do plan to be part of its life, don't you?"

"You know I'm not the kind of person to shirk my financial obligations."

"Oh." Isabelle picked up one of the lemon cookies. "Is that what the baby is? A financial obligation?"

Leave it to Isabelle to get to the heart of the problem, he thought. "No, of course not. I'm just not sure how much I can offer at this point. Financially I'll make sure he lacks for nothing."

"I'd certainly hope so, though that isn't exactly what I had in mind when I asked if you wanted to be part of the baby's life. Writing a check every month doesn't qualify as involvement, Wes."

Involvement. The very sound of the word carried weight.

"There are things far more important than college trust funds. A child needs more than things. It needs parents. Love. Preferably loving parents who love each other."

The nagging guilt that had plagued him ever since he first suspected Justine's baby might be his revved into a higher gear. He thought about the awesome, humbling feeling he'd experienced when he'd felt the baby moving inside her.

"I understand the concept, and I'm sure that I'll love it, but I'm not sure I have what a child—what anyone— needs. I do have a reputation for being a selfish son of a gun, just like Dad."

Some emotion Wes couldn't identify flickered in Isabelle's eyes. "You sell yourself short. You're nothing like your father." After a second's hesitation, she added, "Thank God."

"I never knew you disliked Dad," Wes said.

"I didn't *dislike* him," Isabelle corrected. "I just didn't have much respect for him. He had a fine mind for business, but he was a weak, wishy-washy kind of man otherwise. I swear I never knew what Pamela saw in him, other than his obvious good looks. Believe me, you're nothing like your father." She reached out and gave his hand a maternal pat. "You have a lot to offer a child. But more important, there's so much a child can give to you that you need."

Wes frowned. "Like what?"

"A sense of who you are, for one thing."

"I know who I am. Weston Grayson, II, Esquire."

"That's who you are professionally. But who are you? Lonely aspiring artist, or loner? Both. But why? Because Justine Sutton hurt you badly and you're afraid it will happen again? Is that why you never went through with any of those marriages you planned? Or do you hole up in that cabin out on the lake because your father belittled everything you did and you felt you never quite measured up? What's behind the aloneness, Wes? Fear of failure?"

Wes listened. He didn't like what he heard, but he

knew Isabelle was right. "Dad did mess me up royally, didn't he? And you're right. Justine was the reason I didn't go through with any of the wedding plans. But it wasn't fear of getting hurt that stopped me. It was because none of those women were Justine."

"Ah!" Isabelle said, smiling. "If you keep digging, you eventually get to the truth. You love her, don't you?"

"Love? I'm not sure I know what that is," he denied, fearing it was a lie. "I don't want to shock your sensibilities, Aunt Isabelle, but it's great sex. I want her like I've wanted no other woman."

Isabelle smiled again, her rouged cheeks resembling wrinkled crab apples. "Trust me, I know all about sex. And that's not a bad place to start. As for what love is, it's feeling empty when you're away from the other person."

Empty. Lord, he did feel that. Had ever since she left him so long ago.

"It's knowing they understand you and that you understand them. Not that you have to agree. But you understand."

Justine had understood him perfectly back then. They hadn't always agreed on how best to handle things, but he reasoned that, if anything, age would have brought more wisdom.

"It's not being able to wait until you see the other person again. It's laughing together. Talking together."

The way he felt right now. Anxious to drive to Donovan's to see her, but uncertain what he'd say when he got there. He thought of all the times they'd spent at the cabin, locked away from the real world—talking, sharing hopes, dreams, fears.

"It's fighting and making up. It's complex, Wes. But

let me tell you this. If Justine is the reason you never married another woman, I'd say that what you feel for her is love. And if it's love, you owe it to yourself to marry the woman and give that baby a mother and father.''

There it was. The word he'd been afraid to contemplate. Marriage. Though he'd known it was an option, he'd been too afraid of failing to give it any serious consideration.

He was selfish. He knew that. He liked his solitude. Needed it. A wife and baby would demand a commitment. Time. He imagined having someone in the house. Unfamiliar noises. Crying. Conversation. The thought was intriguing as well as intimidating. Justine was a creative person and understood the creative mindset. Surely they could work out something—if it meant building a studio where he could go to paint and she could get away to write her songs.

Whoa! Was he actually considering offering marriage to Justine?

Yeah. He was. "So you think that if I love her, I should marry her?"

"I certainly do."

"What if she says no?"

"If she loves you, why would she?"

"What if she doesn't love me?"

"You won't know until you ask her, will you?" Isabelle said with a lift of her dark, drawn-on eyebrows.

"Tell me what a baby can give me that I need so desperately?

"The unconditional love Phil never did, never could because he was too in love with himself. A sense of who you are, and what your real reason for being is.'' Isabelle gave his hand another pat. "If you're worried about a baby taking up the time you could be painting, he will. But I promise you that it will be a fair trade-off, and if you want to paint, you'll find the time, even if you have to work around dance recitals and Little League.

Justine, Sophie and Molly called it a day at five, Sophie and Justine agreeing to be back early the next morning to finish. With any luck at all they could. Sophie went home to wait for Reed's call, and Justine went back to Donovan's. There was plenty left to eat, even though they'd sent much of the food to the shut-ins around town. Surprisingly, Justine found she was hungry. Maybe there was something about expending all that emotional energy.

She was filling a paper plate to pop into the microwave when she realized Wes hadn't come as promised. Considering the emotion-packed day she'd just spent, it wasn't surprising that other things had occupied her mind.

Actually, it was probably best that he hadn't showed up. She'd rather talk to him without Sophie and Molly around, especially since she had no idea what he wanted to say to her. Now that her mind wasn't occupied with thoughts of Gene's perfidity and Molly's paternity, she let her thoughts wander to what might be going through Wes's mind, but with Wes, who knew?

The phone rang, and she picked it up on the second ring.

"Hello."

"Hi."

Wes. "Hi."

"Have you had dinner?"

"No. I was just getting ready to warm up some leftovers."

"Why don't you drive out here? I'll throw a couple of steaks on the grill. We'll talk."

He didn't sound angry or confrontational. He sounded sexy and…mellow, she thought. The idea of sharing a meal with him was both tempting and frightening. What if he was luring her there just to soften her up and then tear her heart to shreds by demanding some kind of arrangement with the baby that she couldn't live with? What if she couldn't act normal around Wes, knowing his father was Molly's dad?

But it was Wes, and she was leaving soon, and who knew when she'd see him again or under what circumstances? "Sure," she heard herself say. "That sounds great. Give me time to get cleaned up. All that packing up is dirty work."

"An hour?"

"Make it forty-five minutes," she said.

"See you then," he told her and hung up.

Justine turned off the phone and stared at it for a moment before setting it on the counter. What had prompted Wes to call with a dinner invitation instead of his just coming over and talking to her as they'd planned? Had he come up with some sort of legal document that would outline the role he intended to play in their child's life? Something in black-and-white that spelled out exactly what his obligations would be, something to satisfy the lawyer in him—a certain amount of money in exchange for a certain amount of time? Did he hope that plying her with food would make her more agreeable to his offer? More important, would the offer be something she could live with?

Chapter Eight

Justine showered, applied fresh makeup and spritzed on an old-fashioned rose scent. Then she put on a bright floral-patterned dress that in her opinion made her look like an elephant in a field of exotic flowers but that everyone else claimed was very flattering.

She made the drive to Wes's place on Crescent Lake in less than ten minutes. She saw him out back of the cabin as she pulled down the lane that meandered through a stand of pine and hardwoods. Hearing the car, he turned and watched her until she was out of sight. There was something intense about Wes whatever he did, something that made her tingle with awareness at the same time she suppressed a thrill of misgiving.

She got out of the car, took a small box from the back seat and went around back of the cabin.

"Hi."

"Hi." He didn't quite smile, but she thought she saw

a hint of pleasure in his eyes as his gaze raked over her from head to toe. He put down the glass of tea in his hand and hurried toward her. "You shouldn't be carrying that."

"Better to carry it in a box than on my thighs," she said, as he took it from her. When he looked at her questioningly, she said. "It's a double-fudge cake and peanut butter pie. I remembered you liked it, and I certainly don't need it. I had a really nice salad that had hardly been touched, too. I thought it would be good with the steaks."

"Great. My lettuce had turned to mush in the crisper drawer, so I was just going to open up a can of something." He smiled and Justine's heart took a nosedive. "I did put a couple of potatoes in the oven right after we talked, so they should be ready by the time the steaks are."

"Sounds wonderful. Is there anything I can do to help?"

"Everything's under control," he said, setting down the box and motioning to a weathered Adirondack chair that sat on the flagstone patio. "Have a seat."

She slanted him a wry smile. "If I sat down in that, you'd need a crane to get me out."

"The swing then," he said, waving a hand toward a porch swing set on a four-by-four A-frame.

Justine sat down on one side of the swing.

"Spiced tea?" he asked.

"Sweet or unsweet?"

"Now what Southern boy do you know who drinks anything but sweet tea?" he asked with another smile and an exaggerated accent.

My, she thought, she could get positively drunk on

those smiles, as potent and heady as they were. "Sweet, then."

He put some ice from an ice bucket into a mug and filled the glass, adding a sprig of mint. "A trick I learned from Aunt Isabelle," he told her, handing her the glass.

To her surprise he settled down next to her in the swing. She scoured her mind for something to say, uncertain she wanted to talk about what they both knew she'd come there to talk about.

"How did it go today?" he asked.

"What?" she'd been so focused on trying to come up with a conversation topic, she was at a loss as to what he was talking about.

"Going through your mother's things."

"We didn't finish," she told him. "But we made a considerable dent. We're packing up the things we want and marking other items for either Mama's church or Goodwill to come pick up."

"Your sister is keeping the house, then?"

"For the time being." Justine wondered what Wes would say if he found out Molly was his sister, too. The thought gave Justine a weird feeling. She wondered how Wes could have turned out so well when his father was obviously not cut from very fine cloth. She pushed thoughts of Phil Grayson from her mind. She couldn't handle that just now. Not with Wes sitting next to her.

Thinking about all she and Molly had been through that afternoon, Justine was suddenly glad Wes knew about the baby. What would happen between them was an unknown, but she didn't see how anything he might suggest could be any worse than what had happened to Cassidy and Molly. To find out as an adult that your father was someone other than who you thought him to be had to be devastating, even if, as in both cases, the trade-off was for the better. If nothing else, Justine reasoned, Wes finding out about the baby now had saved a lot of potential heartache and bad feelings in the future.

"You aren't saying much. Tired?" he asked when she added nothing new to the conversation.

She turned and saw him watching her, an expression that could only be translated as tenderness in his dark eyes. That emotion coming from Wes was startling. She'd seen passion in his eyes. And seduction. As a teenager she'd seen that desire and a passion of a different sort, a determination to do better than his father, excitement over the prospects of the future. Sorrow. Despair, even. But never this aching tenderness. It stole her breath and her voice. She nodded.

"I imagine it's been a stressful day."

You have no idea know how stressful. "It has," she agreed, her voice barely audible.

"You'll fell better once you eat." He stood. "I imagine the steaks are about ready."

They were, and Wes set about getting the plates and utensils set up. He went inside and brought out the foil-wrapped potatoes along with containers of butter and sour cream. When everything was to his satisfaction, he went to the swing and held out a hand to her.

Feeling awkward and self-conscious and very aware of his masculinity, she placed her hand in his and felt the tingle all the way to her toes.

He helped her to her feet. "That dress is great on you."

A compliment? It was almost too much. She struggled to overcome her confusion at this new side of him.

"I tell everyone I look like an elephant trying to hide in a patch of flowers," she told him.

His gaze clung to hers. He reached out and tucked a flyaway strand of hair behind her ear. "A very pretty elephant."

"Don't," she whispered with a slight shake of her head.

"Don't what?"

"Don't flirt with me. It makes me uncomfortable."

He regarded her, a contemplative gleam in his eyes. "We sort of bypassed that phase of our relationship, didn't we? We went straight to sex both times."

His brutal honesty made her face flame with color.

"When we were kids, I remember us having some heavy discussions about our problems, our hopes and our insecurities." He seemed determined to have his say no matter how embarrassed it made her. "I remember us making out when we weren't talking, but I don't remember us flirting. And there was certainly no flirtation going on between us in February, was there?"

"No," she said in a soft voice.

"That's a shame. I like seeing you a bit flustered the way you are now. Blushing. Maybe flirting is something we ought to work on, even if it is like closing the gate after the cows get out."

Justine opened her mouth to ask him what he meant, but he touched her lips with his fingertip, letting it linger longer than necessary. "Later," he told her. "Our food's getting cold. I don't like to brag, but I cook a mean rib eye."

He guided her to the glass-topped table and helped her into the chair. The next few minutes were spent putting the condiments on their potatoes and salad. Justine popped a piece of steak into her mouth and proclaimed it delicious. They ate in silence. Considering her apprehension about what it was Wes might propose about their baby, Justine was surprised at how hungry she was.

"I like women with healthy appetites," he told her.

"I'm eating for two," she said, recanting the stock reply of the always-hungry pregnant woman with a hint of asperity.

"Don't get testy," Wes said. "I'm one of those men who finds it very irritating for a woman to order the most expensive thing on the menu then push it around on her plate. It isn't the money. It's the wasting of good food."

"I wouldn't have thought that would have been something that would bother you."

"What?" he asked with a smile. "Because I was brought up with plenty of money? My mother's family got their money the hard way, and we were taught to save by my grandparents after she died. How do you think some of these wealthy people got their money? It's because they're careful with it." He looked thoughtful for a moment. "At least the first generation is. My experience is that after that, thrift seems to go downhill with each generation."

They managed to get through the meal with small talk, and when they'd both finished, Wes asked her which dessert she preferred. "Neither. I'm stuffed. You're right. You do cook a mean steak."

"Just one of my many talents," he told her in a pseudo-smug tone.

"Speaking of talents, I don't suppose you'd let me see some of your paintings?"

He leaned forward and propped his arms on the table,

regarding her with a considering expression. "I'm not sure I know you well enough for that."

She cocked an eyebrow. She knew him well enough for intimacy. Knew him well enough to mother his child. But not enough to look at his painting?

"You know how personal the creative process is. I'm not sure I know you well enough to open myself up for any criticism you might have. It's still too early in our relationship."

"I understand," Justine said. And she did. "Is that what we have between us? A relationship?"

Wes nodded. "A strange relationship, I guess, but for lack of a better term, I guess that's what it is. At least for now."

"I don't follow you," Justine said.

"I know. When are you going back to Nashville?"

The sudden switch in topics caught her off guard. "Soon. We should finish up the house tomorrow. After that, there won't be anything to keep me here."

"What if I gave you a reason? Would you stay?"

Justine's heart began to pound. Reason or ultimatum? Her heart told her Wes wasn't the kind of man to ply a woman with sweet talk and food and then go for the jugular, but her mind argued that he was an all-powerful Grayson, a successful attorney, used to making demands and used to getting what he wanted.

"That would depend on the reason, I suppose," she said, choosing her answer with care.

"What about marriage?" Wes asked, resting his forearms on the table and leaning toward her.

Justine felt as if the ground had just opened up and she'd fallen into a whirlpool of feeling. Had she heard correctly? Had Wes just mentioned...

"Marriage?" she echoed.

"Yeah, marriage." The intensity in his eyes told her he was dead serious.

"You want to marry me?" The words came out in a breathless squeak.

He blew out a harsh breath and straightened. This was no easier for him than for her.

"Let's walk," he told her, getting to his feet.

Justine rose and followed him.

"Honestly, I'm not sure I want to get married at all," he said, heading across the sloping lawn to the long pier that jutted out into the lake. He gave her a sideways glance. "I have a feeling I won't be very good at it, but we have made a child together, and I feel very strongly that I should be part of his—or her—life. That would be next to impossible with us living so far away from each other."

Their footfalls thudded hollowly on the wooden planks of the pier. A portion of her brain noted that there were a couple of black swans cruising the lake, and a camouflage johnboat bobbing in the water next to the dock. But her awareness was only peripheral. Most of her thoughts were focused on Wes's admission.

She had to admire his honesty. There was no pretending that what they felt for each other was love. In short, he was stepping up to the plate, taking responsibility for something he'd done, pure and simple. As surprised and even thrilled as she was, Justine was just a little peeved, too.

"Why don't you just move to Tennessee?" she said, as they came to a floating dock with a four-foot railing around it.

He looked surprised by the suggestion and gestured toward a wooden chair. "My work is here."

Justine chided herself for her sudden irritation and

could have cut out her tongue for asking him the waspish question. His offer of marriage was more—much more—than she'd expected. What on earth did she want him to do? Get down on his knees and make a declaration of undying love? Still, as unfounded as her feelings were, his offer still rankled as much as it pleased. They were both at fault. Why was she expected to make the concessions?

She sat down and met his gaze with a steady I-am-woman look. "And my work is in Nashville."

"I thought about that," he said. "You don't punch the nine-to-five time clock the way I do—even though I do plenty of work at home. I know you travel, but that would be out for a while, and I know you need somewhere to…practice. I was thinking we could build us a big studio out back, one with an upper level so I could paint and a studio with whatever equipment you need to practice your recordings or cut your demos. You could fly back and forth when you needed to be in Nashville in a hurry."

Justine's irritation vanished. She'd expected an argument from him, rife with lawyerese and filled with convincing reasons why it would make more sense for her—a woman—to make the move. Instead, he banished her concern with the obvious solution. He would build a studio for her. As simple as that. She was both touched and impressed by the suggestion. Sometimes having lots of money could solve what seemed to be insurmountable problems.

"And would this be a real marriage?" she asked. "We'd share…a bedroom?"

Wes sat down on a bench pushed against the dock's railing. He clasped his hands together and leaned back, letting them rest on his hard middle. He exuded cool confidence, except for the hint of uncertainty in his dark eyes.

"Of course we would," he told her, a crooked smile claiming his lips. "Can you imagine us living in a house together with all the little day-to-day intimacies and not wind up sleeping together? I can't. I want you too much. I want you right now, if the truth were known." Justine's gasp of surprise didn't even slow him down. "Even with you pregnant, I'd like to take you inside and make love to you all night. Does that make me demented, sick or what?"

Justine's mind whirled with surprise and awareness. "Why would you think you were any of those things? I'm pregnant, Wes. I don't have a terrible disease, and I'm not fragile, so sex is fine, though I'm rapidly approaching a time I should abstain until after the baby is born."

"So if we're going to do it we should do it soon, huh?" he asked, a teasing light in his eyes, something else she couldn't recall ever seeing.

"I don't want to get married just for the baby, not even to give the baby two parents. He can have two parents if I moved here and we didn't get married."

"It wouldn't be the same."

She shook her head. "I don't know. There's way too much divorce. People who truly think they love each other, people who do truly love each other wind up in divorce court every day. Without love, we have two strikes against us going in. As my mama used to say, two wrongs don't make a right."

He leaned forward, resting his forearms on his knees and refusing to meet her gaze. "Love is highly over-rated."

"Are you saying you don't believe in love?" she asked, appalled.

"Not at all. I think a lot of people fall in love and stay in love the rest of their lives. I know enough to know that love waxes and wanes with situations and that love changes as life molds us. But that first flush of awareness and rapid heartbeats and that physical thing, that changes. Sometimes it's up, sometimes it's down. No one could maintain that level of emotion day in and day out. They'd die. And I believe something else."

"What?"

"I believe that when you're in one of those down times, and things are getting to you, and life is mundane and troublesome, you can look across the room at the person in your life and look at the way his or her hair grows or the shape of their hands or whatever and fall in love over and over again."

Justine was more than amazed. Glancing away from him, she stared out over the softly rippling water with the gently bobbing swans and the turtles resting on fallen trees without really seeing anything. Wes's outlook on life and love so closely mirrored her own that he might have been looking around in her mind and her heart.

What he was talking about was exactly what had happened to her in February. She'd opened her dressing-room door to him, and all the old feelings for him, feelings she thought had died years before, feelings she believed were nothing but a part of some special memories, had come rushing back, and she'd found herself loving him all over again. Fast. Hard. Forever? Probably.

As if he were too restless to sit, Wes rose and turned,

clinging to the railing of the deck and looking out over the water. "I think there's something more important than love," he said, when she didn't comment.

He'd surprised her again. What could possibly be more important than love?

"Commitment," he said, even though she hadn't yet asked the question. "A lot of people enter the race, but not all of them finish the course." He turned to face her, leaning against the railing. "I believe commitment is what's behind every successful business venture, every successful relationship—whether it be friendship or marriage. I think commitment is what gets marriages through those down times when things get ho-hum and mundane and everything that can go wrong does. And I want you to know I'd be very committed to this marriage."

"Does that mean that even though there is no love between us there would be no other women, not even in the mundane times?"

"Yes."

He was certainly making all the right sounds, she thought. "Why?"

"Why?" he asked.

"Yeah. Why would you want to make this sort of promise when you don't love me? Why take yourself out of the singles game when you don't have to?"

"Because it's never been a game I played very well," he told her. "Regardless of what you think, there isn't a never-ending line of women to my bed. There have been some women, but not as many as you may think. I almost married three of them, but in the end I couldn't, because the closer the wedding came, the more certain I became that it wasn't right."

"And this is? How do I know you won't back out on me at the last minute, the way you did them?"

"I wasn't willing to make the commitment to them, and in my heart I knew it. I am with you."

"Because of the baby?" she asked, trying to understand, knowing that her and her child's future happiness depended on complete understanding of exactly where this relationship was headed, if she did take him up on his offer.

"No." In a familiar gesture, he stuck his hands in his pockets and gave a slow shake of his head. "Because I've never been able to forget you."

The admission stole Justine's breath and her ability to reason. All she could do was stare at him, while her heart whispered that this was what she'd missed when he'd first suggested they get married.

"You said something before about me not loving you. I'm not saying that what I feel is love. I've never been close enough to the emotion to recognize it. But there is something between us, Justine, on my part anyway. It's strong, and it hasn't gone away, and it's more than sex. Maybe it's tied to the way you made me feel back when we were kids."

"How did I make you feel?" Justine asked, awed by his honesty and his admission.

"You gave me a sense of self-worth my father took away."

"You did the same for me," she said, knowing it was time for her to start making some concessions herself. "You never made me feel as if I was less than human just because I came from the wrong side of the tracks. You treated me like an equal, like my opinions were worth something."

"They were. You always seemed so wise, and you

were so grounded in what you believed about people and situations. It was impossible for me not to believe, too.''

"I guess that came from my mama," Justine told him, realizing for the first time how much her mother's basic tenets had influenced her. "She always said that life wasn't necessarily fair and that no work was lowly if it was honest. She taught us to give a fair day's work for a fair day's wages, to treat others the way you wanted to be treated and that money didn't make a person good or give them character. She also believed that there was some good in every bad person and some bad in every good man.''

"That's pretty sound thinking.''

Justine felt her throat thicken with emotion. "And, despite the life she lived with my stepfather, she was an eternal optimist.''

"There's nothing wrong with that.''

"No. More of us should be that way.''

Neither of them said anything for a moment. "What about you?'' Wes asked at last.

"What about me?''

"You've been asking me some pretty pointed questions. Would you be willing to make the commitment? Would you be faithful?''

Justine's first reaction was anger. How dare he question her faithfulness. She'd never been promiscuous!

Wes doesn't know that. He should, she thought. But then, he probably based his feelings on what he read in the tabloids, just as she'd based hers on the gossip that came from the Lewiston grapevine. Yet, even though he was considered quite the ladies' man, according to Wes, he was anything but that. Gossip was gossip, no matter what the source. The question for them both, then, was whom did they believe?

Wes. She knew him to be honest, and he had no reason to lie about his past, so when he said there had been women, but not as many as she might imagine, she believed him. For that same reason she believed that he'd be faithful to his wedding vows. She certainly would be. She'd seen too much misery caused by broken vows and broken homes to ever want to be responsible for it herself.

"Of course I'd be faithful. I believe that's what marriage is all about."

"Commitment," he said.

She nodded. "I guess so."

"So what do you think?" he asked. "Shall we announce our engagement and let the chips fall where they may?"

"You and me? Together forever? Making a home for our child and building a lasting relationship?"

"Yeah."

"Do you like baseball?" she asked suddenly.

"I was a helluva pitcher in high school," he told her. "I might have done something with it in college, but my dad didn't approve, so I didn't play. Why?"

"I love baseball, and I have this yen to be a Little League mom."

Wes smiled. "I can see it. Maybe I'll even coach."

Knowing they'd just passed some invisible line, Justine smiled back. "Lewiston will have a field day with this one. Heck, the whole country will have a field day."

"What do you mean?"

"We're going to be splashed all over the tabloids and fanzines," she told him. "Your privacy is going to be a thing of the past, and you're going to get your fifteen minutes of fame whether you like it or not.''

"I don't, but if you promise it will go away, maybe I can stand it.''

"We'll be a hot topic for a week or two, tops.''

"Okay.'' Neither of them spoke for several seconds, then Wes said. "Unless you want a new one, I'll get my mother's engagement ring out of the safety-deposit box.''

"You'd give me your mother's ring?''

He shrugged, the elegant lifting of his shoulders that signified the picture of refined indifference. "Why not?''

Why not, indeed? "I'd love to have your mother's ring,'' she told him.

"Good. We'll break the news to the paper, set the date and see about getting you moved and the studio started.''

"About that…'' Justine paused, unsure about how to proceed. "I'm not trying to be greedy or hard to get along with, but do you think we could convert the cabin into a studio and build us a new house? I mean, the cabin is pretty small for a full-time family, and…'' *And I'm not sure I could live there with the memories of what happened there, even though some of it was good, very good.* "…I'm making good money right now. I'll pay half.''

Wes thought about that for a while. "Actually, that's a pretty good idea. I'd been toying with the idea of building another place, but there never seemed to be any big rush, since I was by myself. But I can see that two more people would make things a little crowded, especially, as you say, on a full-time basis. So let's start thinking about what we want, where we want to build.''

"I'd like to build it here on the lake. I'll bet it's a great place to create."

"It is," Wes said, nodding and letting his gaze sweep over the peaceful panorama before him. "And when the muse flies off to parts unknown, I get in the johnboat and fish for a while." He brought his gaze back to her. "Do you fish?"

Justine smiled. "No. But I was never afraid of crawly things growing up, so I'm not averse to learning."

"Good."

Justine pushed herself to her feet and stretched the kink out of her back. It wasn't the marriage proposal of her dreams. There was no dewy-eyed romance, no flurry of expectation, no thrill of happiness. This was more like a business deal pounded out over a conference table. Still, as unromantic as it was, she was marrying the man she loved, so, no matter what the terms, she'd take it. More than happily. "So I guess it's official."

"Not quite," Wes said. "Come here."

The look in his eyes set her heart to racing. She recognized that heat. He was going to kiss her. She knew it as certainly as she knew the sun would set in the west. Without taking her eyes from his, without answering, she closed the distance between them.

When she was no more than two feet from him, Wes reached out and put his hands on her shoulders. Sliding his palms up and down her arms, he urged her closer.

"Do you have any idea how gorgeous you are?"

Heart beating a wild, pagan rhythm, she shook her head. She knew she was pretty, but gorgeous?

"Amazing." He stepped even closer, until her expanding belly touched his hard middle. "A kiss will make it official," he said, in a voice thick with need. "Don't you think?"

"I don't know. Do you seal all your deals with a kiss?" she teased.

A smile slipped onto his beautifully shaped mouth. "Hardly. Most of the deals I cut are with good ol' boys whose biceps are bigger than their IQs, or with the D.A. You've seen Trevor North. What do you think?"

"I think you have a sense of humor, and that surprised me."

"Well, I don't often let it show," he said, lowering his head. "Because there hasn't been much funny stuff in my life."

"Sophie says babies are better than cartoons," Justine said, his mouth a hair's breadth from hers. "So all that is about to change."

"I hope so."

He swallowed whatever reply she was about to make as he claimed her parted lips with his. Justine's hands moved from her sides to his chest. She felt his heart pounding beneath her palms. Emboldened by the effect she seemed to have on him, her arms slid up around his neck and she parted her lips farther, encouraging the invasion of his tongue.

He didn't disappoint her. Each stroke fanned the embers of desire that the memories of their time together had kept smoldering for seven long months. She didn't know how long they kissed, but it was long enough for her to think that if what they felt wasn't love—and she knew that this wasn't that emotion—it would do until the real thing came alone. She dared to hope that with the commitment they'd promised it would. Didn't they deserve love after what life had put them through?

She felt his hands move to her breasts and gave a little moan. Wes deepened the kiss, his hands molding, shaping. "So soft," he whispered against her lips.

This was getting out of hand, she thought, even as a bolt of molten desire shot through her. She didn't suppose it mattered under the circumstances. Except it mattered to her. Somehow she knew she couldn't let Wes make love to her again until they were married. Call it a warped sense of right and wrong, but it was how she felt. Or maybe it was that she felt awkward and self-conscious with the fact that she was no longer slim and shapely. Whatever, it was time to call a stop before it was too late.

"Wes," she murmured, pulling away.

"What?" he looked at her with desire-glazed eyes.

"We should stop."

"Should we? Why?"

She gave a little shrug. "Because it doesn't feel right," she told him.

He looked into her eyes for long moments, then nodded, like a man who's finally seen the light. "Okay. Somehow I sense that this had more to do with some embarrassment on your part at the thought of my seeing you in less than a drop-dead-sexy light than it does with any right or wrong."

"Maybe," she conceded with a nod.

"I can buy that," he told her, sliding an arm around her shoulders and starting up the pier. "But it's something you're going to have to get over real soon, because I don't plan for this to be a long engagement."

Chapter Nine

As they walked back to the house, Wes could almost feel Justine's weariness. She'd had a very emotionally and physically trying few days. Losing her mother, dealing with the condolences of strangers and shifting through Ruby's material possessions and whatever memories they held had to take its toll, especially since Justine was bound to tire more easily than she might if she weren't pregnant. To receive an unexpected proposal of marriage on top of everything else had to have her mind spinning.

"I'll help you clean up, and then I think I'll head home," she said when they reached the patio.

"I'll clean up. You go. You look about ready to drop," Wes told her.

"I am. It's been a rough few days." Her words echoed his earlier thoughts. "Sophie and I are supposed to meet Molly early tomorrow morning to try to finish up.''

''I'll get the ring and call the architect tomorrow. And I'll tell my family what's going on. I'm sure Lara will write up something for the newspaper.''

He saw the uneasiness in her eyes when she said, ''What do you think your family will say about this?''

''It's none of their business, but I don't think anyone will be too surprised, since most of them know about the baby.''

''If anyone had told me you were such a blabber-mouth, I'd never have believed them.''

''I'm not a blabbermouth,'' Wes said in his own defense. ''I just happen to come from a family of very astute people. When they back me into a corner with suppositions and theories or plain old facts, I don't lie.''

''Neither do I.''

''Then we have that in common, too.'' He put an arm around her shoulders and guided her around the house to her car. ''We're going to have to get rid of the Mustang and get a bigger car. A minivan, or an SUV.''

''Why do I have to get rid of my car? Why don't you sell the roadster?''

Wes grinned. ''Ouch! A woman who isn't afraid to speak her mind.''

Justine didn't smile back. Her demeanor was one of complete seriousness. ''I'm not the same kind of woman my mother was, Wes. I happen to think that marriage is a two-way street. I think there are certain roles each partner plays, but that on occasion the lines between those roles blur. I don't mind making part of the money if you don't mind changing diapers. We're both going to be working, so I suggest that we share the child care. I'll cook if you'll cook. I'll be your partner, but I won't be your doormat. I'll stand up for what I believe are my rights, and if you don't like that, then we're off to a bad start.''

Wes listened, amazed and exhilarated by the challenge in her voice. The next thirty years promised to be exciting. ''Actually, I think I like the idea of a woman who talks back. It'll keep me sharp for the courtroom. And I have a solution.''

''What?''

''We buy a minivan and keep the roadster and the Mustang.''

''Works for me,'' she said.

''And I do like the fact that you stand up for what you believe. It ought to keep things from getting boring.''

''I can't see life with you ever getting boring,'' she told him.

''Ditto. One more question. Who's going to clean and do laundry?''

Justine thought a moment. ''I vote we hire someone.''

The sound of a car approaching put the conversation on hold. They both turned to see a silver Lexus coming down the lane. Wes cringed inwardly. What the hell was Rowland Hardisty doing out here?

The car pulled to a stop and Rowland got out, resplendent in the Brooks Brothers suit he'd worn to the funeral. There was a cocky swagger to his walk and a determined—almost malevolent—gleam in his eyes as he approached.

Though Wes and Reed were as close as brothers and their fathers had been close friends, Wes had never cared much for Rowland, whom he considered arrogant,

domineering and vain. Rowland was the kind of guy
who could make Genghis Khan look like a choirboy.

"Good evening, Rowland. What's on your mind?"
Wes asked. There was no sense beating around the
bush.

Rowland glanced at Justine. "I need to talk to you."

"I'll go," Justine said, starting off.

"No need," Rowland said in a smooth voice.

"What could you and I possibly need to talk about?"
Wes asked.

"Getting mixed up with the wrong kind of woman."

"Exactly what does that cryptic statement mean?"
Wes asked, sticking both hands into his pockets. He
suspected that whatever it was Rowland had come to
say, it wouldn't be to his liking.

"After your mother died, Phil went through women
like tissues. And he always went for the wrong kind.
He wasn't as…discriminating as he might have been."

Justine made a sound, and Wes glanced at her. Her
eyes were wide with disbelief and pain.

"I saw the two of you at the cemetery," Rowland
continued, gesturing toward Justine. "No man puts his
hands on a woman the way you did Justine without
there being some intimacy between them."

Wes couldn't deny Rowland's observation and didn't
want to or intend to. "I don't have to justify my actions
to you or anyone else, Rowland. I'm over twenty-one."

"Maybe so, but your father wouldn't like your taking
up with her."

Wes laughed, a bitter sound, even to his own ears.
"Did you ever know me to do anything my father ap-
proved of? If there is something between me and Justine, it's no one's business but ours. We're both single
adults, and in case you've forgotten, my father is dead."

"Did she tell you she was sleeping with him while she was sleeping with you?" The question was delivered in a cold, flat voice.

Justine drew in a strangled breath. Wes glanced at her, struggling to make some sense of the ugly accusation. Justine and his father? Ridiculous! But she'd grown deathly pale, and the gaze that clung to his held an emotion that could only be called horror. She took a couple of steps to the car, leaning against it as if she needed the support.

Wes's skepticism faltered. He looked from her to Rowland. The expression in his eyes was one of callous disregard tinged with satisfaction. It was a look Wes had witnessed often through the years. It made no difference how badly his words or actions might hurt. All that mattered was that Rowland satisfy whatever evil impulse or perverse sense of righteousness that drove him. That he do whatever it took to manipulate people and lives to his liking.

"You're crazy," Wes said. He'd always had Reed's dad pegged as someone whose success as a surgeon had more to do with challenge, skill and the need to lord it over lesser doctors than it did over any real desire to minister to his fellow man.

"Am I? Ask her."

It was hard to doubt the confidence in Rowland's voice. Wes turned to Justine again. The misery in her eyes was clouded with guilt. An image flashed through his mind—Justine and his father…together. It was impossible to comprehend, but the expression on Justine's face told him there was some truth to Rowland's statement.

"Is this true?" he asked, incredulity lacing his voice.

Justine's hand went to her lips and her eyes filled with tears. "It isn't what you think."

"A simple yes or no, Justine," Wes said, his pain deepening. "Did you sleep with my father?"

The tears overflowed her lower lashes and trickled down her cheeks. "Yes, but—"

Wes saw red, and his mind reeled. "You think you can justify it?" he yelled.

"No! I just—"

"I'll leave and let the two of you hash this out," Rowland said, happy to go now that he'd accomplished what he'd set out to do.

"You do that," Wes snarled. "And if you ever set foot on my property again, I'll have you sent to jail for trespassing."

"Hey, don't be mad at me," Rowland said, throwing up his hands in a "back off" gesture. "I'm only the messenger. If you think this was easy for me, you're—"

"Damned right I think it was easy for you," Wes said. "You relish scenes like this. In fact, I think you like screwing up people's lives almost as much as you do saving them. Well, don't forget that you reap what you sow, Rowland. And your time is coming. Now get out of here."

Rowland turned and retraced a few steps to his car. Breathing hard, angrier than he could remember being in years, Wes watched Reed's father turn the car around and head back down the lane.

"I'm going, too," Justine said, when Rowland's car disappeared around a bend in the road. She wiped at her eyes with her fingertips and turned to open the car door.

Wes grabbed her arm and pulled her around. "Like hell you are!" he said through gritted teeth. He stared into her tear-filled eyes. Her lips were pressed into a tight line, as if she were trying to stop their trembling. "You're going to stay right where you are and tell me how you could be such a lying, scheming..." He paused.

"Slut?" she finished for him, her own anger clearly on the rise. With a sob she raised a fist and struck him on the chest, a surprisingly hard blow. "How can you be such a judgmental jerk?"

Wes snared her wrist in a firm grip. "I'm not judging you, Justine, I—"

"What do you call it, then?" she asked, trying to pull her arm free.

"Stop it!" he commanded. "You'll hurt yourself."

"As if you care," she cried, struggling harder. "Let me go, Wes!"

His hold on her wrist tightened. "You admitted you slept with him. Tell me how you could do that, Justine. Why did you? Were you playing us against each other? Was he better than I was? More experienced? Did he pay you for it?"

She gave a wail of agony and grew still suddenly, as if all the fight had gone out of her. She stared up at him, her eyes drenched with tears, mascara leaving a trail through the whisky-hued freckles that stood out in stark relief against the paleness of her cheeks. Despite his own fury and the pain raging through him, Wes felt as if he'd just kicked a stray puppy. He released his hold on her wrist. She brought up her other hand and rubbed it.

"Like you told Rowland, I don't owe you any explanations for my actions," she said. "Whatever happened between—" she swallowed hard "—between me and your father happened seventeen years ago. It has nothing to do with now. It has nothing to do with you."

"It has everything to do with now and with me!" he bellowed. "That's my baby you're carrying, and I just asked you to marry me. Now I find out you made love with my father."

They stared into each other's eyes for long seconds, both breathing hard, Justine crying. Wes wishing he could.

"Don't worry, Wes. I won't hold you to the proposal. You can keep your freedom and your self-righteousness. And we didn't make love. It was sex, okay. Not even good sex."

"Thanks for that bit of information, but don't you think that's splitting hairs?"

She raised both hands to her head as if it were about to explode and she hoped to hold it together. "I can't do this. I can't."

"Fine, then. Go." Disgust laced his voice. He stepped back and she sat down in the driver's seat, closed the door and put on her seat belt. The engine turned over with the first turn of the key. He tapped on the window and she turned to look at him.

"I'll be in touch," he told her.

She didn't reply, just turned away, put the car into gear and roared away from the house in a cloud of dust and a spray of gravel. Hands on his hips, Wes watched her go. She took the turn at a speed that sent the rear of the Mustang fishtailing in the loose rock, straightened the car out and with a grinding of gears sped out of his sight and out of his life.

Wes watched her go, wondering how things could have gone so bad so fast. How had they gone from planning a future together to bitter adversaries in the span of ten minutes? The answer wasn't hard to find.

Rowland Hardisty.

Wes passed a hand over his eyes as if the gesture might somehow erase the past few moments from his memory. It didn't work. His mind was still filled with tormenting images of his dad and Justine. He remembered suddenly that she hadn't been a virgin that first time with him. His father's doing, or someone else's? Feeling as if he might be sick, he turned back to the house, his movements as slow as those of an old man.

He needed a drink, he thought as he made his way to the kitchen. That would dull the edge of the pain that threatened to consume him. A couple of shots of Jack Daniels. Even a couple of beers. But there was no liquor in the house. He hadn't wanted to be tempted. He'd have to settle for a pot of strong black coffee. He closed his eyes for a few moments and did the deep breathing routine the hypnotist he'd seen had suggested when he'd felt the urge to fall off the wagon. In a few minutes the craving passed.

Thankful that he'd managed to beat back another potentially debilitating fall from grace, he filled the coffeepot with water then took the coffee can from the freezer and measured the grounds into the filter, all on automatic pilot. What would happen now? Marriage to Justine was impossible. He wasn't sure he could ever touch her without remembering…yet even as he thought it, he realized that the mental image brought no new pain.

He felt empty inside. Hollow. As if his heart had been jerked out by the roots. There was no pain, no anger, just the emptiness and a bleak certainty that happiness, perhaps the first real happiness of his life, had been snatched from him by the cruel hand of fate in the guise of Rowland Hardisty.

Mission accomplished. Rowland could hardly hold back a satisfied smile as he got into his car and left Wes and Justine fighting like two alley cats. It wasn't that he felt any pleasure from his actions...well, maybe just a little. Wes had never been anything but a disappointment to Phil, and Justine Sutton was nothing but the daughter of a slut and a slut herself, despite whatever she'd accomplished since she left Lewiston. If Wes felt guilty for knocking her up, he could send her a check every month. There was no sense in him getting personally involved and doing something stupid like marrying her.

Wes might be furious now, but when he got over his anger and really gave the situation some thought, he'd see that Rowland was right. Why, he'd come to him one day and thank him. Rowland knew for sure that Phil would thank him for putting an end to whatever it was brewing between those two. And that's why he'd done it. As a good deed for an old friend.

Justine clung to the steering wheel with a white-knuckled grip. She could hardly see the road for the tears. Could hardly breathe for the harsh sobs wracking her body. She was going too fast, she thought, as she made the curve in Wes's drive and the rear end of the car slid sideways, but she had to get away from the condemnation in Wes's eyes, away from the condemnation in her own heart.

Impossible. It had haunted her for seventeen years, and all this newest wrinkle would do was elevate the pain and guilt to a higher level. She would never forget, and thanks to Rowland Hardisty, neither would Wes. She pressed harder on the accelerator and had the passing thought that she should probably turn on her headlights. The day was drawing to a close, and the shadows in the wooded area were settling in.

Why had Rowland done it? Because he liked making people miserable? She knew from what she'd heard her mother say that he thought he was the next thing to God. Did he twist the truth and engage in his hurtful manipulations because he was truly so self-confident that he thought he knew what was best for those concerned and intended to make sure things came out the way he envisioned them? Or was there a more sinister side to his actions? Was he simply a self-confident man who liked using his power? She didn't know. All she knew was that he had ruined her life, probably forever.

She hit a pothole and momentarily lost control of the car. There would be no marriage between her and Wes now. Her baby would have no live-in father. There would be no new house, no studio. No sharing of chores. Just a future filled with the heartbreak of a lost love and a child who would remind her of that love every time she looked into its face.

A fresh rush of tears blinded her, blurring the sudden movement from her peripheral vision as something darted out in front of the car. She jerked the wheel to try to keep from hitting the deer, knowing instinctively what it was, knowing as she wrenched the steering wheel she was doing the wrong thing. There was no thought of her own harm, only that of her baby.

A blur of brown and long, nimble legs flashed before her, and beyond that, trees. A sudden rush of panic and terror. The sound of her own voice screaming in denial…

Later she would think that she could recall the moment of impact and the splintering of the windshield, but then, she reasoned, maybe what she remembered was just the shattering of her heart.

The forlorn hooting of an owl nudged aside the darkness enveloping Justine. A hard cramp in her abdomen banished the rest of it. Fighting the nausea pushing its way up her throat, she forced her eyes open and found herself face-to-face with an airbag. Fragments of memory came rushing back, tumbling over one another. Wes. Angry. The deer. The smug expression on Rowland Hardisty's face. Driving fast. Too fast. She knew she was hurt but not sure how badly. She tried to move and there was an excruciating pain in her arm. She heard herself gasp, and the darkness closed in on her again.

The next time she came around it was almost fully dark. She was groggy, but knew of some elemental level that she'd crashed the Mustang. She tried to clear her mind of everything and assess the situation, but it was next to impossible when she could hardly breathe for the airbag that held her all but motionless. How long had she been here? Long enough for darkness to have covered everything. She knew she was hurt on a gravel road that no one but Wes traveled with any regularity.

She fumbled her seat belt free and started to reach for the door handle, only to find that trying to move her arm caused excruciating pain. Broken. It didn't matter. She couldn't get out, anyway. The driver's side of the car was flush against a tree that blocked her exit and bowed the door so far inward it pressed against her side.

A panicked whimper escaped her, followed by a

groan of agony when another pain knotted her belly. The baby! She had to get out of the car somehow. Had to get help. The sound of a phone ringing haltered her hysteria. A phone? How? Her cell phone! Stretching to the right and fighting the pain in her back, she groped in the seat for her purse, praying it hadn't fallen to the floorboard. Thankfully, her fingers encountered the slender strap almost immediately. Justine curled her fingers around it and dragged it to her side. Groping inside, she pulled out the still-ringing phone, somehow managing to flip it open with one hand and pull out the antenna with her teeth, praying all the while that whoever it was wouldn't hang up, praying she wouldn't pass out again.

"Hello." Her voice sounded hoarse and whispery, as if she had a bad case of laryngitis or it hadn't been used in a long time.

"Justine!" Sophie said. "Where in the world are you? I tried calling the house, and when I didn't get an answer, I checked with Molly, but she didn't know where you were, either. We've been worried sick, so I—"

"Sophie, listen." Something in Justine's husky plea halted Sophie's words.

"What is it?" Sophie asked, alarmed.

"I…I had a car accident."

"Car accident! Dear God! Where are you? The hospital? Are you all right?" Sophie's concern erupted in a flurry of questions.

"I'm on the road from Wes's place. A—" she bit back a moan "—a deer jumped out…in front of me. I can't…get out of the car, Sophie. The baby…" Her voice trailed away and a sob followed. That was quickly followed by another pain. She clenched her teeth around a groan.

"Don't move!" Sophie commanded. "I'm hanging up and calling the ambulance right now. They'll be there in a few minutes. Hold on, Juss." The line went dead. Justine had enough of her wits about her to turn the phone off before darkness swooped down on her again.

Almost thirty minutes after Justine left, Wes heard the sirens in the distance but paid no attention to them. The highway beyond the gravel road that led to his house was a busy one, and there was a nasty curve just past the turnoff to the lane. It never occurred to him that it might be Justine.

Rowland Hardisty was at home, getting ready to take his wife out for a rare evening together when the emergency call came. The ambulance service had received a call from Sophie saying that her cousin, who was about seven months pregnant, had crashed her car on Crescent Lake Lane. The hospital was letting Rowland know so that he could be there scrubbed and ready when the ambulance came in.

He hung up and broke the news to Grace, who only nodded. She was used to having her plans interrupted by Rowland's profession.

"We need to talk," Grace said.

"Later," Rowland said, grabbing his keys and heading to the door. He was already thinking about Justine's accident—Sophie had said it was her cousin and that she was pregnant, so it had to be Justine. She and Wes must have had a heck of an argument after he left. Rowland could picture it. Justine leaving in tears, knowing her life and her plans to snare herself a wealthy husband were ruined. Crying. Losing control of the car.

He felt genuine remorse, but not for what he'd done. After all, all he'd done was tell the truth in an effort to stop an old friend's son from making the biggest mistake of his life, something he hadn't been able to stop his own son from doing. Wes was angry with him now, but he'd thank him later.

Rowland was genuinely sorry if his actions were the reason behind Justine's accident. Sorry she and her baby were hurt. His only intentions had been to stop the relationship between Justine and Wes from developing further. But since she was hurt, he would do everything in his considerable power to save the baby and bring Justine back to health.

"Rowland."

Grace's voice stopped him at the door. He turned, scowling. She was dressed for dinner—some fancy new place in Little Rock—and looked very nice. "What?" he snapped. "I have an emergency."

"I know." She twisted her fingers together. "I was going to tell you at dinner, but since that's off, I'll tell you now."

"Tell me what?"

"I saw an attorney on Friday. I filed for divorce."

If it hadn't been one of the most profound moments of Grace Hardisty's life, it would have been the most comical. The expression on Rowland's face was one of stunned disbelief. For once in her life, she'd succeeded in shaking him up. He was so self-absorbed, he hadn't seen it coming. Still, it wasn't Rowland's style to admit defeat.

"Don't be ridiculous, Grace. You can't divorce me. You'll be the joke of the town."

"I already am."

"We'll talk about this later," Rowland said, frowning.

"Fine," Grace told him with a slight shrug of her shoulders. "But you won't change my mind."

"Good God! You haven't found someone else, have you?" he asked, taken aback by her resolve.

"Yes," she said. "Myself."

Rowland shook his head. He didn't understand. "You're having some sort of midlife crisis," he murmured. "Some chemical imbalance or something. I'll run some tests tomorrow."

"You'd better go," Grace told him. "We'll talk about this when you have more time."

He gave her a final, pensive look and left her standing in the foyer. Grace locked the door behind him and went upstairs to get ready for bed, pleased that she'd managed to rattle his implacable composure. Sorry that it had taken her more than forty years to do it.

She'd put up with that self-absorption far too long, doing her best to be the dutiful wife and mother. She'd grown accustomed to her life and her needs playing second fiddle to her husband's, but she'd never liked it.

She'd had a scare—a lump in her breast a few months back that she hadn't even told Rowland about—and even though it had been benign, it was the wake-up call she'd needed. She'd taken stock of her life, the things she'd accomplished, which, beyond wife, mother and volunteer work, were nonexistent.

She'd thought of the things she'd always wanted to do, things that Rowland would forbid because they didn't fit with her role of doctor's wife. She'd realized—no, she'd acknowledged—that she was tired of taking a back seat in her husband's life and sick to death of his pompous attitude and his affairs. Mostly, she was tired of the way he treated people, especially Reed and his new wife and daughter. If Lara and Belle had no objections, why should Rowland?

Grace found Sophie bright and caring. More important, she was crazy about Reed. And Cassidy was a delightful young woman, smart, pretty and with a level head on her shoulders. Grace's only sorrow was that because of Rowland and Hutch Delaney's actions seventeen years earlier, she'd been denied a lovely granddaughter for sixteen years.

But no more. She had a new life planned, and there was no room for Rowland Hardisty or his ego in it.

Rowland was waiting when the ambulance pulled screaming to the emergency room entrance. As the paramedics wheeled the gurney into a room, Rowland barked a few orders that were immediately obeyed and began his examination of the patient. She wasn't Justine Sutton at the moment. She was just a patient who needed his skill and expertise. The scene with Grace was far from his mind.

Justine opened her eyes. He thought he saw a flicker of surprise in hers. He felt her hand take hold of his wrist, her grip surprisingly strong.

"Don't hurt my baby."

What was she talking about? He'd never hurt her baby. He'd taken an oath to save lives, not harm people.

"Hurt me all you want," she said in a groggy voice. "But don't hurt my baby."

Rowland felt something unfamiliar knot up inside him. Perhaps, for the first time in his life, he felt a twinge of guilt for his actions. Then Justine gave a little groan of pain and everything was forgotten except the moment and learning the extent of her injuries.

Like Grace's announcement about filing for a divorce, Rowland would think about that flicker of guilt later.

Wes paced the floor, thinking about his argument with Justine. He knew he'd come down on her pretty hard, but he hadn't been prepared for the pain Rowland's announcement had brought. Excruciating pain. Pain that told him that his feelings for her were deeper than he imagined, that it was truly love he felt. With that love came not only the need to protect, but a possessiveness and jealousy he'd never experienced. He knew he'd have to temper that feeling, or a modern woman like Justine would run as fast and as far as she could. But on the other hand, he was just getting used to the whole gamut of emotions this new role of prospective husband and father brought.

Damn Rowland Hardisty! And damn Justine. How could he have been so far off in his assessment of her character?

A more important question might be why did she do it, Grayson?

True. Had she found an older man more attractive, suave? Wes knew his dad had been a handsome man; in fact, if the number of women who'd chased him was any indication, he'd still been attractive when he died six years ago. But the age difference was something that was hard to ignore. As an adult, Wes realized his dad was a womanizer and that he'd been unfaithful to his mother before her death. Knowing that, he understood how his dad had been captivated by Justine. But what had made him attractive to her? He needed to remember that she'd been sixteen, poor and impressionable. Had he given her gifts? Made her promises? What?

Wes paced and drank coffee and longed for a drink…anything to numb the ache in his heart. A sudden thought struck him. Was his father involved in any way with her leaving town without a word? He swore.

Does it really matter after all this time? Probably not. Knowing wouldn't change things, but his very nature demanded that he know all the lurid details so he could better wallow in his misery.

The phone rang. He approached it warily. He didn't want to talk to anyone right now, but the caller ID showed it was Lara, and she usually only called when she had something important to say.

"Hello."

"It's me," Lara said. He heard the breathless note in his sister's voice.

"Hey, Sis. What's up?"

"I called to tell you that Justine had an accident on the way home from your house. She's in the hospital."

Chapter Ten

Wes's heart broke into double time. A memory of Justine leaving, tears streaming down her face and driving way too fast flashed through his mind. "Accident?" he echoed.

"Evidently she lost control of the car on the gravel."

"Is she okay?" Wes asked, knowing it wouldn't have happened if they hadn't argued so bitterly.

"Sophie says they're waiting to hear the extent of her injuries."

Wes had a vision of Justine's beautiful face cut by a shower of glass. Another thought hit him like a punch to the gut. "What about the baby?"

"We haven't heard. I understand Rowland called in Tom Kincaid, since he has more experience with that sort of thing."

"Rowland!" Wes snapped. "Why is Rowland taking care of her? I don't want him touching her!"

Lara didn't say anything for a few seconds. No doubt she was trying to understand what caused his outburst. Finally she said, "He's taking care of her because he was on call, and you know he's the best surgeon around."

Wes felt the blood drain from his head and fought back an unfamiliar and unmanly wave of dizziness. "Surgeon!"

"Look, I don't know what's going on," Lara said in a tone she usually reserved for recalcitrant students and had never used with him. "But you need to calm down. You know as well as I do that Rowland and Tom are the only two doctors in town, and they're darned good, both of them. The hospital has top-notch equipment and the best nursing staff in this part of the state. If Rowland and Tom can't handle it, they'll fly her to Little Rock."

Wes knew she was right, but his heart was overriding his common sense, and his heart was breaking at the thought that Justine was hurt, maybe badly. He also knew enough to know that the baby was in jeopardy simply because Justine was.

"You're right," Wes said to Lara. "But Rowland Hardisty is part of the reason behind the accident."

"Do you want to explain that?" Lara asked in an incredulous voice. "No. Never mind. It's none of my business, and I'm not sure I want to know. Suffice it to say, after being married to Reed for eleven years I'm familiar with the way Rowland operates, and I'll bet he said something to drive a wedge between the two of you."

"That's the gist of it," Wes said. "Are you at the hospital?"

"Everyone's here but Cassidy and Belle," Lara said.

"They're at the house. Sophie called Molly. She's on her way."

"I'm coming in. You have my cell phone number. If you hear anything before I get there, call me."

"I will."

Wes started to hang up, then thought of something and called his sister's name.

"Yes?"

"Worst-case scenario. What if she goes into labor? Will the baby make it?"

"I'm not a doctor," Lara said, choosing her words carefully, "and I'm sure there are a lot of factors that can make a difference one way or the other. But if I had to hazard a guess, I'd think the chance of the baby surviving would be good."

Wes closed his eyes in a moment of thankfulness. "Thanks, Sis."

"Sure."

"I'll see you in a few minutes."

"Be careful."

"Always."

Wes found everyone in the first-floor waiting room. Lara rose and crossed the room to hug him. Donovan said hello. Sophie sat across the room on a burgundy settee, regarding him with a considering look. Not judging. More of an evaluating sort of expression in her eyes. Justine's younger sister sat next to Sophie, who held Molly's hand in a tight grip.

"How is she?" Wes asked of no one in particular.

"We haven't heard anything since I called," Lara said, looping an arm around his. "Rowland and Tom are both with her."

Wes glanced around the small room, searching for a

chair, and Sophie asked Wes if he remembered Justine's sister.

"It's been a long time," he said, forcing what he hoped passed for a pleasant smile and extending his hand in greeting. "Other than the funeral, I believe you had dog ears and braces the last time I saw you. You reminded me of Lara at the same age."

Molly Malone sucked in a little breath, and her eyes widened in surprise, but for the life of him he didn't know what he'd said. Who knew what wayward memory a seemingly innocent comment might bring to mind?

"Did they give you any idea when they might know something?" he asked.

Lara shook her head and gave his arm a comforting pat. "Why don't you sit down and try to relax. Molly and I are going to the snack bar and see what the machines have to offer. Do you want something?"

"Some coffee if they have it."

Lara took orders from everyone in the room, and she and Molly left clutching dollar bills in their hands. Wes tried to sit, tried to relax, but it was impossible with his mind filled with gory images of Justine…hurt and bleeding.

Please let her and my baby be all right. The prayer, the first one he recalled uttering in years, became a chant that rang through his mind, a mantra against all the terrible things he knew could be wrong. Never a religious man, Wes still believed in an all-powerful deity. He believed that God was good, and, from his childhood Sunday school lessons, he knew that God sent blessings even to the unrighteous. He also remembered the passage that read, "the Lord giveth; the Lord taketh away." But surely God wouldn't bring Justine back into his life and give him the promise of a child and then snatch them both away, would He?

Unable to bear the thought, Wes leaped to his feet and went to the doorway, positioning himself where he could see anyone coming or going. She had to be all right. Had to. Funny, he thought. A little less than two hours ago, he'd been so angry with Justine he couldn't think straight. Now, faced with the possibility of losing her, whatever it was that had happened between her and his father became insignificant. It was strange how things changed with perspective.

Now nothing Rowland said mattered in the least. What mattered was that Wes loved Justine and that he wanted the baby they'd made together. He wanted to marry her and make a home for the three of them, the way they'd planned before Rowland had come with his vicious story.

As if thinking his name had conjured him from the dark depths of Hades, Rowland, wearing his familiar green scrubs, stepped through the double doors at the far end of the hall and strode purposefully toward him. It might have been Wes's imagination, but there was a subdued expression in Rowland's eyes, a weariness to his step. Wes's heart hammered in renewed fear and panic.

"How is she?"

He and Rowland might have been the only two people on the first floor. On some level, Wes realized that the others had risen, eager for news but willing to let him do the talking.

Rowland stopped a few feet away. "She has a broken left arm, some facial bruising, some cuts and a couple of cracked ribs. She'll be fine."

"The baby?"

''Is in distress.''

''Distress? What does that mean?'' Wes asked, feeling his own distress magnify.

''Justine has gone into premature labor. Ideally, since he's still so small, we'd try to stop the labor, give him some steroids to build up his lungs and hope to go a few more weeks, but under the circumstances, Tom feels that a C-section is our best chance, and frankly, so do I.''

Chance. Our best chance. For what? Wes asked himself, even though he knew the answer. A caesarian section was their best chance of saving the baby. Wes grabbed the door frame to steady himself.

He heard Sophie say something and felt Rowland reach out and take his arm. Wes looked from the surgeon's long, sensitive fingers to his face. A face that held genuine concern, something Wes never recalled seeing on Reed's dad's face in all the years he'd known him.

''Take it easy,'' Rowland said. ''He's going to be little, but little ones make it every day.''

''Do it.''

''Tom's scrubbing up now.'' Rowland's gaze swept the occupants of the waiting room. ''I'll do the surgery. He'll assist. I'll let you know how things are going.''

Rowland turned to go and paused when he saw Lara and Molly returning from the snack bar, their hands full of colas and candy. He stared at them for a moment, then with a brief ''hello'' went back through the double doors.

While Wes was pondering the thoughtful expression he'd seen on Rowland's face, Molly and Lara asked, ''What did he say?''

The question came from them simultaneously. Something about the concern on both faces held him captive, and he looked from one set of brown eyes to the other. A feeling of déja vu swept over him as he noticed the slant of dark eyebrows, the aristocratic shape of both women's noses, the sweep of cheekbones and the stubborn set of two chins. It was the same feeling he'd experienced the day a few months earlier when he'd been at Lara's house watching Belle and her new friend, Cassidy, swimming.

Now, as it had then, incredulity washed over him in staggering waves. Was he the only one who could see how much Molly Malone looked like Lara, or is that what had caused Rowland to hesitate for those few seconds? Dear God, how could anyone look at them and not realize the same blood flowed in their veins? As farfetched as his mind told him it was, Wes had little doubt he'd stumbled onto another family secret.

"Are you okay?"

"What?" he asked. His sister's question brought him back to earth with a start.

"You looked as if you'd seen a ghost or something," Lara said.

He forced a smile. "I'm fine."

"What did Rowland say about Justine?" Molly asked. Her frowning eyebrows and downturned mouth were a carbon copy of Lara's.

Wes gave them a condensed version of what Rowland had told him.

"They'll both be okay," Lara said in a positive tone.

"I hope so," Molly said in a disconsolate sigh.

Wes watched as Lara followed Molly into the room and started dispensing the snacks. Minutes that seemed like hours passed. Wes walked the floor, his mind divided between concern for Justine and the baby and his recent discovery. Why hadn't he seen the resemblance before? Probably because he'd never seen the two side by side before. They didn't exactly run in the same circles. In fact, he could probably count on one hand the times he'd seen Molly Malone around town through the years.

A lot of things made sense now, like why his dad had left the house on Logan Lane to Opal Malone when he died. Like everyone else in town, Wes had imagined the gesture was one of good will, his dad being the generous benefactor to a grieving widow with three kids at home. But it hadn't been generosity that motivated his father. Wes knew that now. It had been guilt, pure and simple.

His dad had had an affair with another man's wife and had gotten her pregnant. Wes remembered the Opal Malone from his youth. She'd been a looker, and with his dad's proclivity for women, it was no surprise that he sampled all the wares Lewiston had to offer.

Wes recalled Gene—a thin, wiry man who dressed in starched jeans and cowboy boots and pearl snap Western shirts. He'd driven eighteen wheelers for a living and liked to play the ponies at various racetracks across the country. It would have been easy for Opal to get away to meet his dad without getting caught. Had Gene Malone suspected anything? Had he known the baby wasn't his? Did he even care? He wasn't the most sensitive guy in the world. Hadn't he abandoned his family when Molly was small?

Another question nudged aside the hows and whys. What should he do with his suspicion? He'd have to tell Lara. It was only a matter of time before someone else figured it out, if they hadn't already. Lara should be told, and Isabelle, of course. In fact, Isabelle prob-

ably already knew. She kept her fingers on the pulse of
the town and pretty much knew what was going on with
its residents.

"Hello, Wes."

The greeting derailed Wes's thoughts. He turned to
see Tom Kincaid standing a few feet away.

"How is she?"

"Justine is fine. She came through it like a champ.
You have a son, Wes. Congratulations."

Wes didn't feel like congratulations. He was still too
worried abut that status of the baby's health to care
about its sex. "How is he?"

"Small, but remarkably strong. We're sending him
by ambulance to Little Rock, where he can get more
specialized care. Neither Rowland nor I have the knowledge to handle things if an emergency arose."

"Can I see him?"

"In a few minutes. I'll send the nurse down just before they're ready to leave."

"When can I see Justine?"

"She'll be in recovery for an hour or so. You can
see her when we assign her a room."

"Thanks, Tom." Wes said, thankful that everything
was okay with both the baby and Justine.

"Sure."

Wes watched the doctor retrace his steps to the double doors, then he turned to face the people in the waiting room. Forgetting they'd heard every word he and
Tom Kincaid had exchanged, Wes said, "It's a boy."

Lara erupted from her seat next to Molly and hurried
across the room to hug him. Sophie followed suit and
then Molly. Donovan shook his hand and asked when
they could expect their cigars. Fatherhood was already
making its demands. There were cigars to buy, flowers

for Justine, a trust to set up for the baby's—what would they name him?—college. He had to make some changes to his will and see the architect and get the house underway, and...

Wes's mental list came to an abrupt stop.

He could do some of those things, but before he could start the house, he had to apologize to Justine and make her understand that he'd been hurt by Rowland's claim. He had to tell her, to make her see that, faced with the prospect of losing her, it didn't matter.

"Justine."

A pleasant female voice called her name. Justine tried to answer, but she was so sleepy she couldn't get her eyes to open or her mouth to work.

"Justine? Can you wake up just a little?"

This time her eyes fluttered open. A round-faced woman with a salt-and-pepper hair and wire-rimmed glasses smiled down at her. "How are you doing?"

"Fine. Where am I?"

"You're in the recovery room."

The words triggered a memory, and it all came rushing back—the dinner with Wes, Rowland's arrival, his devastating news and her flight from Wes that had ended with her Mustang crunched against a tree. A portion of her brain that functioned normally despite the pain medication told her she'd survived.

"My baby..." she said, licking her dry lips and fighting to stay awake. "What about my baby?"

"A boy," the nurse said.

Justine was too relieved that her baby was alive to care if it was a boy or girl. A wave of darkness washed over her. "Is he...okay?"

"He's fine."

She felt her eyelids drift shut and was too tired to try to open them. "Can I see him?"

"Later. You go on back to sleep now."

The gentle command was unnecessary. She'd already drifted off.

At some point Justine was aware of being wheeled down the hall. She asked where they were taking her and drifted off as soon as they told her they were taking her to her room.

The next time she awakened it was to the sound of a masculine voice. She forced open her eyes and saw Rowland Hardisty standing over her. Dread filled her, even though she couldn't put her finger on why.

"How do you feel?" he asked.

Her tongue skimmed her dry lips. "Okay. May I have some water please?"

"No water," Rowland said. "Only ice chips." He fed her a few spoonfuls, which were wonderful. Exhausted, Justine closed her eyes again.

She was about to drift off when she heard him say, "This is my fault, but I want you to know that I'm going to do everything in my power to fix things."

Justine had no idea what he was talking about, but murmured that it was okay. Then she let herself be carried away on medicated dreams.

The baby was on his way to Little Rock and a topnotch neonatal man. Rowland and Tom were both satisfied that they'd done the right thing. Tom had gone home, but Rowland had lingered, wanting to make sure Justine was okay and to let her know he intended to make restitution for his wrongs.

He'd left her room a chastened man, uncertain she

was awake enough to understand. It didn't matter. He did. Ever since she'd begged him not to hurt her baby in the emergency room, Rowland had been taking a long hard look at himself. He knew he was a type A personality, a workaholic who wanted things done his way when he wanted them done. But much of his success in the operating room depended on things happening when and how he knew they were supposed to.

He even knew he had a problem with ego, though he chose to ignore it. He wasn't unaware of the whispers that followed him and knew he'd been accused of having a God complex. He didn't deny it. He was good at what he did, and he knew it. There was something heady about facing a critical situation and knowing that life and death were in your hands. Something intoxicating that came from snatching a patient from the door of death.

The problem was that he'd let his satisfaction become pride and his vanity become narcissism. Somewhere along the way he'd gone from being a good surgeon to a great act that he had to follow with each and every succeeding patient. He was nothing like Tom Kincaid, who would have practiced medicine in some remote village in South America or Africa without pay or fanfare.

Unlike Tom, Rowland had traded his humanity—if he'd ever had any—for conceit. He'd taken his success and knowledge in the operating room into every aspect of his life, believing he knew what was best for everyone and in every situation. He'd manipulated, harassed and cajoled his life into one where he was the master puppeteer, and if he couldn't pull someone's strings, that person became someone to crush...like his own son.

Sometime shortly after Reed and Lara had married,

Reed had developed a backbone and had refused to knuckle under to Rowland's wishes or demands. In retaliation, Rowland had done his best to make him feel less a person, to make his life miserable in small ways. Unfortunately, even that backfired. Reed continued to live his life the way he wanted and didn't seem to mind the widening chasm between them, especially since he'd married Sophie Carlisle.

Rowland knew he had been unreasonable in his attitude toward Sophie and Cassidy, but it rubbed against the grain that Reed was determined to marry Sophie despite Rowland's warnings. It also chafed that his and Hutch's machinations when Sophie had come up pregnant seventeen years earlier had been found out. Guilt, Rowland realized, was great motivation for continuing the bluff.

Guilt. A tremendous guilt when Justine had begged him not to hurt her baby. Guilt that prompted this inward look. An inspection that had long been needed. One that was turning up things said and done that Rowland had conveniently forgotten or refused to think about.

Like Grace. Grace had filed for divorce, and he'd had no idea she was unhappy. No, that wasn't true. He'd known she was dissatisfied with her life for years, but had countered her pleas for some changes with his stock reply. She'd known there would be demands on his time when she married him—such was the lot of a small-town physician.

He tried to imagine life without Grace and couldn't. Though he'd never told her—perhaps because until this moment, he'd never realized it—she was the mainstay of his life, his center. All soft words and classy elegance and a good heart, she was not only the epitome of a doctor's wife, she was the very essence of the Southern gentlewoman. She'd been a good and faithful wife, a devoted mother to Reed, and was probably first in line to follow Isabelle Duncan's footsteps for being the town matriarch. She was respected and loved and known to do for the poor as well as the wealthy, yet none of it had gone to her head...as it had his.

Needing to assure himself Grace was still at home, Rowland left word at the nurses' station that Justine could have visitors for short periods of time and instructed the head RN to call if anything changed. Then he headed down the hall, wanting nothing but to go home and spend some time thinking. It was time to make some changes in his life—if it wasn't too late. He would do his best to heal the rift with Reed and his new family. He would try to fix things between Wes and Justine. And he would do his best to piece together his broken marriage.

He had his work cut out for him, he thought, as he stepped out into the darkness and started toward the car, which sat beneath the circle of illumination provided by one of the two lights in the hospital's small staff parking lot.

Rowland was halfway to his car when he heard something like a shot ring out in the darkness. Almost simultaneously he felt a sharp pain in his side. There was no time for surprise. He was unconscious before he hit the asphalt.

Micah Lawrence was one of the first to hear the call that someone had been shot in the parking lot of the hospital. The call had come in from a group of teenagers who were taking a friend home. One of the kids, who just happened to be looking out his window, had heard what sounded like a shot and thought he saw someone lying in the parking lot. They'd checked and found the victim. One had called 911 from his cell phone while another ran inside to tell the emergency-room personnel.

Micah radioed that he would take the call and asked for backup. When he arrived, Tom Kincaid and three nurses were already wheeling the victim through the emergency-room doors.

"Who is it?" Micah asked, falling into step behind the quartet.

"Rowland Hardisty."

Micah swore. Rowland wasn't his favorite person in Lewiston, but he was a damn fine doctor, and it would be a shame if the community lost him. "How bad is he hurt?"

"I'm not sure yet," Tom said, glancing at Micah as he walked alongside the gurney. "I've got to check him over." Outside the doors of the emergency examination room, he stopped momentarily and said, "Would you like the honor of telling Grace what's happened?"

"No," Micah said, taking off his hat and slapping it against his thigh. "But I will."

"Good." With a weary smile Tom disappeared through the doors.

Micah drove straight to Grace Hardisty's house. She wasn't there. Now what? He wondered. Maybe he ought to try Reed's place. Sure enough, her silver-gray Lincoln was sitting in the driveway. Micah got out, rang the doorbell and waited. Reed's sixteen-year-old daughter came to the door, her hair wrapped in a towel. Her eyes widened when she saw him.

"Hello…Cassidy, isn't it?" Micah asked with a smile.

"Yes, sir," she said without smiling.

"Is your grandmother here? I need to speak to her."

"Yes, sir. Just a minute." She turned to go up the stairs, then turned back and said, "Would you like to come in?"

Micah took off his hat and stepped through the doorway. "Thank you."

In less than a minute Grace Hardisty came down the stairs, a questioning look on her patrician features. Sophie and Cassidy—both wearing frowns—stood looking over the railing at the top of the stairs.

"Hello, Micah," Grace said, her pale-blue eyes shadowed with worry. "Cassidy said you wanted to see me. Is something wrong?"

"Actually, there is," he said. "Someone shot Rowland out in the hospital parking lot a few minutes ago."

The color drained from Grace's face. "Shot! Who would want to…" She broke off, possibly recalling that Rowland wasn't the most popular man in town. "Is he…" Her voice trailed away, as if she couldn't bring herself to say those words, either.

"He's alive. Tom was getting ready to check him over. He doesn't know how bad it is."

Sophie came down the stairs, Cassidy trailing behind her. "We just left there less than half an hour ago," she said. "Rowland said Justine could have visitors, and we all agreed that Wes was the logical one to go in, at least for tonight."

"Is he…do you think Sophie should call Reed to come home?" Grace asked. "He flew to St. Louis right after the funeral."

Micah had forgotten. "That's up to you. Maybe you should see what Tom has to say and then decide."

"That's a good idea, Grace," Sophie said with a nod. "Let me get my purse, and I'll drive you to the hospital." She cast a look at Cassidy. "Go run a brush through your hair. You need to come with us."

Cassidy looked as if the request pained her, but she didn't say anything.

"Do you have any idea who did it?" Grace asked, as Cassidy went upstairs to do her mother's bidding.

"None," Micah said.

Wes was sitting beside Justine's bed when he heard what could only be called a quiet commotion in the hall. Rising, he poked his head out the door to see what was going on. Two nurses had their heads together in a hushed conversation. His interest piqued, he closed the door behind him and sauntered to the nurses' station.

"What's going on, Betty?" Wes said to a woman he'd gone to high school with.

"Someone shot Dr. Hardisty as he was going to his car," she said, her eyes filled with disbelief.

As much as he disliked the man, Wes didn't wish him any harm. "Is he all right?"

"We don't know," Betty said. Tom's with him now. His family was coming in as I started up here."

"I'll go down and see them," Wes said.

While they waited for word from Tom, Grace filled Wes in on what Micah had told them. The official family notification over, Micah was out helping the police round up and question the teenagers and the neighbors who might have heard something.

When Sophie posed the question of who might have

done it, Wes didn't even miss a beat. "Carl Lawrey. He had motive, means and opportunity."

"Carl Lawrey?" Sophie said. "Isn't that the man who's on trial for spousal abuse?"

"Yeah," Wes said. "The no-account scumbag is out on bail."

"But why would he want to hurt Rowland?" Grace asked.

"Because Rowland testified for the prosecution a few days ago. He painted a very graphic picture of all the injuries he's treated the Lawrey family for over the past few years. That alone was enough to send Carl up the river for a long time."

"But why would Carl want to worsen his situation by trying to kill Rowland?"

"Who knows how people like him think?" Wes said. "Maybe he figures he's going to do time, so he should make it really worthwhile. And sometimes people go a little crazy at the thought of going to prison. I do know that Carl's done drugs so many years he's bound to have destroyed a few brain cells."

A sound at the door made them all stop and turn. A nurse in green scrubs stood there, a frown on her face.

"How is he?" Grace asked, her own face gone pale suddenly.

"Tom said to tell you the bullet went through a kidney. He doesn't have the knowledge to do this sort of operation, so he's just getting him stabilized while the helicopter from Little Rock is on the way. The main thing right now is we need some blood. He was out in the parking lot long enough to lose a fair amount. Our reserves are down since the Labor Day weekend, and Dr. Hardisty is AB, a rare type."

"Reed is AB," Grace said.

"But Reed is in St. Louis," Sophie reminded her mother-in-law.

"That's right."

"I'm AB."

Everyone turned toward the sound of the hesitant voice. Cassidy stood there, her hands knotted together, a look of fearful determination on her face.

"We typed our blood in one of my labs last year," Cassidy said. "I'm AB."

"You're too young," Sophie said.

"I'm the same size as you," Cassidy said, "so why should age have anything to do with it? I'm not going to wimp out or anything."

"How old are you?" the RN asked.

"Sixteen."

"Technically she's supposed to be older, but he really needs the blood," the nurse said to Sophie and Grace. "If you'll give your consent, I say we double check the type and make an exception this one time."

Sophie looked at Cassidy. "Are you sure you want to do this?"

"He's my grandfather, Mom," Cassidy said, as if the statement said all it needed to. And perhaps it did. Sophie only wondered why Rowland didn't think the same way.

Chapter Eleven

Wes was dozing in the chair beside Justine's bed when he heard a sound. He awoke instantly. He saw her eyelids open a crack, then a little more. She stared at the ceiling while he stared at her, a prayer of thankfulness running through his mind. Even though the nurses had assured him she was doing fine every time they'd come in to check on her vital signs throughout the night, until now, he hadn't trusted their word. Every time she'd been awakened by one of them, she'd asked about the baby, and when she was guaranteed he was okay, she would drift away again, sleeping off the effects of the anesthetic and the pain medicine.

Now she turned her head and looked around the room. When she tried to move her hands to her stomach, she realized her left arm was in a cast. She made a little noise of dismay and tried to sit up.

Wes's hand shot out and pressed against the shoulder of her good arm. "Lie still."

She turned toward the sound of his voice. "Where am I?"

"The hospital. You had a car accident leaving my house last night."

He knew the exact moment she remembered. Pain replaced the confusion from her eyes.

"It was a deer," she told him, her eyes closing as if they were too heavy to hold open. "I was going too fast, and this deer ran out in front of the car. I couldn't stop."

"Arnold Grimes say it was the biggest buck bagged in this county in the past five years," Wes told her with a smile. "He said he knew a good taxidermist, if you wanted to have the head mounted."

Justine wasn't in any frame of mind to appreciate the irony or the humor. Her eyelids drifted shut again. "What are you doing here?"

Her voice was slurred from the medication, but it seemed she recalled enough to know they hadn't parted on the best of terms. "Keeping you company."

Her eyelids fluttered up, briefly. "What about the baby?"

"You went into labor, probably from the stress of the accident. He was in trouble, so Tom and Rowland thought it was best to deliver him."

"Rowland?" she said with a grimace. "I begged him not to hurt the baby. He didn't hurt the baby, did he?" she asked, her eyes dark with concern.

"No. He didn't hurt the baby."

Now wasn't the time to tell her that Rowland had been shot leaving the hospital and that he was finally paying for at least a portion of his sins.

"Good," she said, and drifted off to sleep again.

The next time she woke up, they went through a different version of the same conversation. Wes knew the drugs were wiping out not only the pain, but her memory, as well. This time she forced her eyes open and said, "He? Then it was a boy?"

Wes nodded, unable to hold back another smile. "He's small, but they tell me he's doing fine."

Justine gave a little moan.

"Are you hurting?"

She nodded.

"Whenever the pain gets bad, push this little button," he said. "It'll give you some medication." He showed her how the morphine drip operated, and in moments she drifted back off to sleep.

By the time they rolled the breakfast trolly around, she'd been awakened by nurses twice more. Both times she asked if she could see the baby and was told the baby had been taken to Little Rock. At breakfast she was still groggy but managed to eat a little Jell-O and drink some juice. Wes was asked to leave while they gave her a sponge bath and got her up to walk.

By the time they let him back into the room, she was exhausted. She turned a weary gaze to him. "Are you lying to me?"

"About what?" he asked, going to stand at the side of the bed.

"The baby. No one will let me see him."

"So you think something's wrong?"

She nodded.

"The medicine is making you forget, Justine," Wes said, unable to stop himself from brushing back a lock of dark auburn hair. "They sent the baby to Little Rock. That's why you can't see him."

"Why?" she asked, alarm in her voice and her eyes.

"Because he's small and needs a lot of specialized care that neither Tom, Rowland or the hospital is equipped to give him."

"But he's okay?"

"He's as okay as a baby his size can be," Wes told her again. "So far he's doing fine."

"Did you see him?"

Wes nodded. Smiled. "He looked like a skinny little old man."

Justine thought about that for a moment, then frowned and said, "Don't hide anything from me. I mean, if something…happens to him, you have to tell me."

"I will," he promised.

Visitors started coming right after lunch. Sophie and Reed, who had flown in from St. Louis on the red-eye, and Cassidy, who was feeling none the worse for having given blood, were her first visitors. They came bearing a box with an exquisite emerald-green gown and robe and another box containing two outfits for the baby. As small as they were, Wes knew they would swallow his newborn son. He cornered Reed in the hallway and was told that Rowland had had surgery to repair the damage to his kidney, but that he was doing fine for now.

Donovan and Lara came bearing gifts as did Isabelle, who brought Godiva chocolates. Molly came alone and could hardly keep from crying as she clutched Justine's hand and tried to talk. The flowers were delivered several arrangements at a time, enough flowers that Justine could have started her own florist's shop.

Gifts arrived, too, both for Justine and the baby. Local people who'd heard the news and were fans sent letters and cards, saying they were praying for her and the baby. Finally, seeing that she was physically and emotionally exhausted, Wes told the nurse not to let any more visitors in.

Assured that she'd be allowed some time to rest, he told her he was going home to take a shower and change.

"You don't need to bother coming back," Justine told him, her eyes shadowed with fatigue and glazed with the effects of the painkiller. "There's no reason to."

"I'll be back."

"Don't you think you're being a bit hypocritical?"

"In what way?" he said, though he knew very well what she was talking about.

"Pretending to care when you really hate me for what I did."

Ah, Wes thought, she'd finally remembered it all. He stuck his hands into his pockets. "Maybe I had a change of heart," he told her.

Her lips curved into a wry, weary smile. "Oh. I got hurt, you suddenly realized you loved me and what a loss it would be not to have me in your life, and you realized what happened between me and your dad isn't really important and you're here to make amends for all the things you said."

He nodded. "Yeah. Something like that."

She closed her eyes and turned her face away from him, as if to let him know she couldn't bear to look at him, the gesture telling him she didn't believe him for one second. "Go home, Wes."

Wes knew he was fighting a losing battle. At the

moment she was too physically fragile for him to argue his case. She needed a few days to get back up to speed, and then he'd make her understand that he meant what he'd said. He did love her, the past didn't matter, and he didn't want to spend one more moment of his life without her in it.

When Wes got home, he showered and changed, and then he called Sophie and asked if he could come over and talk to her. In the days before Chicago, he'd have hit the bottle to dull the pain and fear, but that wasn't an option any longer. For once in his life he admitted he needed some help to get through the next few days. He even admitted that he needed some advice on how to proceed with Justine. He needed to bare his soul, to tell someone about Justine and his dad, and the most logical person was Sophie, who was trained not to let personal feelings get in the way of her professional know-how.

He drove into town, and Sophie met him at the door, assuring him that it was a good time—Reed had driven back to the hospital, and Cassidy and Belle were upstairs listening to a new CD.

"Did you hear about Micah arresting Carl Lawrey?"

"No."

"He questioned some motorists who were in the area at the time of the shooting and got a description of a couple of vehicles that might have been involved. One was Carl's truck. Micah drove out to Carl's place with a search warrant. Carl and his cousins were together, and they were wiped out on drugs."

"Not surprising."

"No. The rifle they used on Rowland was lying on the floor next to Carl. He admitted he did it and said the only thing he was sorry about was that he didn't take better aim, but Larry was driving, and hit a pothole in the street. Micah said Carl is a crack shot and pothole or no pothole it was a blessing he was stoned, or he doubted Rowland would still be alive to tell about it.''

''I'm glad they got him,'' Wes said, following Sophie to her newly renovated kitchen.

''We aren't finished with the house yet,'' she said, urging him to have a seat at the antique wrought-iron table she used for informal meals. ''But it's coming along.''

''It's a great house,'' Wes said.

''Would you like some coffee?''

''Please.''

''Justine and I were talking about building a new one before the accident,'' he said as Sophie started the coffee.

Sophie glanced at him over her shoulder. ''I didn't know the two of you had gotten so far.''

''We were working on it. I convinced her that since neither of us had found anyone to marry in all these years, maybe we should make things legal for the baby.''

''Spoken like someone used to cutting deals,'' Sophie said, with a lift of her eyebrows.

Wes wasn't certain he blushed, but he felt his face grow hot. ''Meaning where was the romance?''

''Yeah.''

He managed a lopsided smile. ''In Chicago?''

''That was sex, not romance, but go on,'' she said, putting a brown filter in the basket of the coffeemaker.

''We both thought it was important to give the baby a stable home, and I was adamant about being part of his life, so we thought marriage made a lot of sense, romantic or not. I believe that commitment is more important than that fickle emotion called love.''

''I tend to agree, but I think love is important, too.''

''You're right, and I wasn't discounting my feelings for her. I did feel something for her, but when you grow up the way I did, how am I supposed to know if what I feel is the real thing? Anyway, I thought what I felt and my commitment to staying for the long haul was enough to base a marriage on.''

Sophie turned on the coffeepot and sat down across the table from him. ''You have a point. A lot of marriages based on nothing but commitment and mutual respect have survived. So what happened?''

''Rowland.''

''Rowland?''

''Yeah,'' Wes said. He brushed a hand over his eyes. ''Justine was just going home, and Rowland came out to the house and said some things about her.''

Wariness entered Sophie's eyes. ''What kind of things?''

Wes pressed his lips together, trying to find the right words to say what he had to say to Sophie about her cousin. Unable to, he pushed back his chair and strode across the room. Sophie didn't prod; she waited

Finally Wes turned and faced her, determination in his eyes. ''You know that Justine and I were…seeing each other back when we were kids?''

''Yes.''

''Well, Rowland told me Justine was sleeping with my dad at the same time.''

Sophie's only reaction was to close her eyes. When she opened them, she said, ''And you felt betrayed.''

''Damn right I felt betrayed,'' he said. ''Wouldn't you?''

"Under most circumstances, yes. What did Justine say?"

"She didn't deny it, and I lit into her. It wasn't pretty."

"And Rowland?"

"He was only too happy to leave. You could almost see him mentally rubbing his hands together." Wes leaned his hips against an old granite-topped kitchen cabinet that had recently been refurbished. "I was rough on her. Too rough, considering all she'd already been through. She said that she wouldn't hold me to the marriage proposal, and she left."

He met Sophie's calm gaze, unaware of the anguish in his own eyes. "She was crying and driving too fast. The accident was my fault, and so is whatever happens to the baby."

"She hit a deer, Wes," Sophie pointed out. "It happens all the time around here and you know it. Don't blame this on yourself."

"But if she hadn't been so upset and distracted, her reflexes might have been faster. She might have been able to control the situation better."

Sophie gave a slight shrug. "Sometimes life hands us situations we can't control."

Wes had the feeling she was talking about something else entirely. To his surprise she got up, went to the phone and punched in a number. "Molly?" she said after a few seconds. "This is Sophie. I know you're busy trying to get things in order so you can leave, but do you mind bringing Aunt Opal's diaries over? Yes. Right now, if you can. I'll be here. Thanks."

Sophie saw the question in his eyes. "There's something in Aunt Opal's diary you need to see for yourself." She gave him a wan smile. "So while we're waiting for Molly, why don't you tell me why—if you have such bad feelings toward her—you've been at Justine's side since the accident.''

''That's the strange part,'' Wes said, the expression in his eyes saying he didn't understand. ''As soon as I got word of the accident and no one could tell me how badly she'd been hurt, all I could think of was that what happened in the past didn't matter nearly as much as the thought of losing her forever.'' He shook his head. ''Something about the idea of her dying put things in perspective.''

''Yeah,'' Sophie said, ''it does.''

''The problem is that Justine isn't buying it. Not that I blame her after the things I said.''

''She's been through a lot the past four days,'' Sophie reminded him. ''Give her some time. When Reed and I were trying to figure out exactly what happened in our past, we would reach some sort of meeting ground and then we'd have something else come along and slap us in the face. We did a lot of yelling and made a lot of accusations we had to live with later. But we were able to work through it because we couldn't ignore one simple fact.''

''Which was?''

''In spite of it all, no matter which of our father's lied, we still cared for each other.''

''I think Justine feels something for me.''

''I know she does,'' Sophie said. Then she smiled. ''The coffee's done.''

By the time they'd finished a cup of coffee, Molly had arrived, carrying the diaries. Molly was surprised to see Wes there and handed over the journals reluctantly. ''Rowland told Wes that his father and Justine were…sleeping together,'' Sophie explained, knowing Molly was wondering what was going on.

Molly gasped. "Why would Dr. Hardisty do such a spiteful thing?"

"Because he's alive and breathing," Sophie said. "I thought it might help if Wes saw what your mother wrote about Justine in her journal."

Molly seemed to hesitate, and Sophie knew she was thinking about her mother's confession that she was Phil Grayson's child, not Gene's and that Wes was bound to see it. Well, fine. He needed to know. Sophie was sick of the subterfuge and the lies. She wasn't like Rowland Hardisty, wanting the truth to come out to cause more pain. She wanted the truth to come out to start a healing. They'd all been lied to, and they had all suffered from the sins of their fathers. It might help Wes to learn that Phil had a few flaws of his own.

"It'll be okay, Molly," she said, her heart convinced she was doing the right thing.

"Okay," Molly said, pulling one of the books from the stack and flipping through it until she found the place she was looking for. She handed it to Wes, who took it with a curt "Thanks."

He read for a moment, then raised his head to look at Sophie. "Are you implying that Gene intentionally sent Justine to my dad for sex?" he asked in an incredulous voice.

"I'm not implying anything," Sophie said. "But that's exactly what he did, according to that diary and what Justine has told us. Evidently Aunt Opal went on a regular basis—at Gene's insistence. But she was still recovering from Molly's birth and couldn't go, so—"

"Wait a damn minute!" Wes said, holding up his

hands in a "stop" gesture. "You're telling me that Opal Malone slept with my father in exchange for the rent?"

"I'm only telling you what Aunt Opal wrote. Keep reading."

He did. It didn't take long. Sophie knew the exact moment he got to the place about Molly being Phil's child. The irritation on his face turned to incredulity. He kept reading. Finally, he lifted his gaze to Sophie. There was no hiding the stupefication in his eyes. Undoubtedly, the picture her aunt painted of his father was one far removed from the image Wes held of him. His gaze drifted from Sophie to Molly, who stood wringing her hands and gnawing on her lower lip.

"To say I'm stunned is an understatement."

"Then you believe what she wrote?" Sophie asked.

He gave a short bark of humorless laughter and gestured toward Molly. "How can you look at her and not believe it? She looks so much like Lara it's uncanny. Even I noticed the similarity, but blew it off."

"I wasn't sure whether to tell you or not," Molly told him. "I didn't want to cause any trouble."

"It isn't any trouble. I'll take a look at what Dad left me and Lara, and see to it that you get your third. We may need a DNA test just for the legalities, but—"

"Oh, no!" Molly cried, mortified by the whole idea. "Tell him that isn't necessary, Sophie."

"It is," Wes said. "If you're our sister, and it seems you are, then it's the right thing to do. Believe me, Lara and I have plenty from our mother's side of the family. She won't mind at all."

"Molly really doesn't want to upset the status quo, Wes," Sophie told him. "I'd planned to let her make the call on whether or not to tell you and Lara, but when I decided you need to see what Aunt Opal wrote about your dad and Justine, it seemed to me you should know the whole truth. The whole crazy scenario makes a little more sense if you know what motivated Gene.''

''Yeah,'' Wes said, but Sophie could tell that none of it really made any sense to him.

''I knew my dad liked women and that there were a lot of them. Aunt Isabelle confirmed that. But I never dreamed he'd get involved in anything like this.''

''Aunt Opal and my mother were both beautiful women when they were young.''

''I remember.'' Wes gave his attention back to the diary for a few seconds. ''So the…thing with my dad wasn't Justine's doing.''

''No. She swears it only happened once. Aunt Opal's diary seems to confirm that.''

''Yeah,'' he said nodding. ''I can't believe he'd do something like that…with someone underage. That's statutory rape.''

''I know.''

''At least now I know why she left town without a word.'' His tormented gaze found Sophie's. ''I'm like Opal. What kind of monster was Gene Malone, anyway?''

''The worst kind. The kind who preys on women and innocent children.''

''Like my dad.''

Sophie didn't answer. She'd presented the facts. It was up to Wes to draw his own conclusions.

''I said some pretty terrible things to Justine,'' he said. ''Do you think she'll ever forgive me?''

''All you can do is ask her.''

Ask her. It sounded simple, Wes thought as he drove home, but before he could ask Justine's forgiveness for the bitter savagery of his accusations, he had to tell his sister about Molly.

Since Lara was back at school, Wes killed time at his house until it was time for her to get home. Then he drove over, the diary in his hand. He wanted to show Lara what he considered proof of Molly's parentage.

Lara greeted him at the door with a warm hug. "What's that?" she asked, indicating the diary.

"Something I want you to take a look at," he said, handing her the diary.

"Okay." She turned it over in her hands, regarding it curiously. "How's Justine?"

"She was doing much better when I left," he said. "I don't think she's taking as many painkillers as she was. She seems more alert."

"Do you want to tell me what happened between you two before the accident?" she asked.

"How do you know something happened?" Wes asked, even though he figured if he was in for a penny, he might as well be in for a pound.

"Because you had a terrible guilty look when you first got to the hospital."

"Can't hide anything from you," he said.

"You never could."

"Except that I was seeing Justine when we were kids."

"Touché. So are you going to tell me or not?"

"Yeah, I'm gonna tell you." For the second time that day, Wes launched into the story about his and Justine's decision to get married and why. Then he told Lara about Rowland's visit and the bomb he delivered.

Lara was as stunned as Wes had been. "You're telling me Justine Sutton slept with our dad when she was sixteen?'' she asked, in a horrified voice. ''I don't believe it. Dad would never do such a thing.''

''Come on, Lara. You know what a womanizer he was, and besides, she admitted it,'' Wes said. ''Then she told me it wasn't what I thought.''

''What does that mean? That he forced her? That it was rape?'' Lara's face wore a look of consternation and disbelief.

''At the time I didn't know what she meant, and I didn't care. I was too mad. It was only when I went to Sophie's that I found out the truth.''

''Wait! I'm confused. I'm assuming Justine left after the argument and had the accident, so you went to talk to Sophie because you were feeling guilty about that.''

''Right.''

''What I don't understand is what Sophie could have told you about Justine and Dad.''

''Sophie didn't tell me anything.'' He pointed to the diary. ''Opal Malone did.''

''That's Opal Malone's diary?''

Wes nodded. He took it from her and opened it to the passage he thought he could recite by heart. ''Read about three pages,'' he said, handing the book back to Lara. ''Read about Molly.''

Lara took the journal, rested her forehead in her palm and began to read. Once she made a sound of disbelief, and once she looked up at Wes with shock-filled eyes. She turned the page and continued. When she finished, she closed the book with a soft slap and slid it across the table with one finger, as if touching it were abhorrent.

There was torment in her eyes. ''Do you believe the part about Dad and Opal and…Molly?''

He nodded. "She looks so much like you it's impossible not to believe it."

Lara thought about that and gave a heavy sigh. "That's why he gave her the house," she said with sudden insight. "Guilt."

"Probably."

Lara sat quietly for long moments, just staring. "Poor Justine," she said, finally. "It must have been terrifying for her. I mean, it seems she was a virgin when…when Gene sent her to Dad."

"Yeah." Another silence stretched between them. "I was hard on her, Lara."

"You were hurt," she told him in his defense. "That's a pretty shocking piece of news to deal with."

"Yeah, but I shouldn't have flown off the handle the way I did. I should have listened."

"Patience has never been your strong suit. Where was Rowland while the two of you were arguing?" Lara asked.

"He just got in his car and left."

"I've never understood why he's the way he is. I do know this. He's given Grace all the grief he's going to."

"How do you figure that?"

"When Micah told her about Rowland being shot, she was at Sophie's breaking the news to her that she's filed for divorce."

"Grace Hardisty filed for divorce?"

Lara nodded. "She'd already told me and Belle."

"But she was at the hospital."

"Oh, she's a classy lady. She'll stand by him during all this. She'll act the part. But I know Grace."

"Maybe his getting shot will cause her to change her mind," Wes suggested.

"Doubtful," Lara said. "Grace is the kind of person who takes and takes and has a hard time making a decision, but once she makes up her mind, she doesn't change it. What we need to hope for is that Rowland getting shot will give him a whole new perspective on the way he meddles in people's lives."

"Maybe it will," Wes said. "But I'm not holding my breath."

Chapter Twelve

On the morning she was to leave the hospital, just two days after the baby's birth, Justine actually thought she might survive. The pain from the caesarian section was manageable with pills, and she was able to get up and down with minimal help. She was ready to leave the hospital but knew she wouldn't be able to manage alone and didn't have a clue as to what she was going to do. Molly had gone back to school. Lara and Donovan and Sophie and Reed all offered her their houses for a few days, but everyone worked, and there would be no one around if Justine needed help. Her best solution seemed to be to go back to Donovan's old place, since he'd be around working at the greenhouses at least most of the time and could keep an eye on her.

While she was pondering her options, Wes informed Tom Kincaid that he would be with Justine, either at Donovan's or his own place. When he told Justine, she told him that was impossible. She couldn't—wouldn't—stay in the same house him.

"I'll make you a deal," he told her. "You don't give me any flak about this, and the first day you feel up to it, I'll take you to see baby."

"You drive a hard bargain."

"I know. It's part of what I do for a living."

She hadn't seen anything yet, he thought. He would make her understand the change in his attitude—the change in his heart—if it was the last thing he did. He would explain that the change had come before he'd learned the truth and that the truth had both sickened and saddened him. Sophie had made him see that dwelling on past mistakes was futile. Nothing could change them. You couldn't take back the things said in anger. But you could put them aside, resolve not to make that same mistake and do what you could to change the future. He knew that to conquer Justine's distrust and anger, he had to win the small battles, to take one step at a time.

"It's bribery," she told him.

"I know."

She regarded him with an icy expression. "You have a deal."

His smile was unrepentant. "I thought so."

While Wes was making arrangements to get Justine discharged, Rowland was being examined by his doctor, who announced that he was doing fine. "You're a lucky man."

Rowland wasn't feeling lucky. When he was awake enough to be aware of his situation, he was feeling sorry for himself. "How do you figure that?"

"You have two kidneys. From what I hear, the perpetrator was a good shot. If he hadn't been whacked out on drugs, you'd be in a casket right now.''

Rowland admitted he had a point.

''And you can thank the doctor who took care of you just after the shooting for some excellent emergency-room care. If he hadn't gotten that blood from your granddaughter to help stabilize your blood pressure, you might have been in worse shape when you got here, which would have made my job a lot harder.''

''My granddaughter?'' Rowland said, frowning. ''They took blood from Belle to give to me? She's too young to give blood.''

''Is Belle the preteen?''

''Yes.''

''Then it wasn't her. It was the other one. The pretty teenager.''

Rowland didn't know if his astonishment showed or not. But he was stunned. Cassidy had given him blood. Why? Rowland didn't try to delude himself. He knew his treatment of her and her mother had been pretty shabby, yet they were both unfailingly polite in return. As he drifted off to sleep, he conceded that they had good manners, even if their ancestry left a lot to be desired.

Sheriff Micah Lawrence sat in front of his television, where the meteorologist was apprising the viewers of possible stormy conditions along the east coast. But Micah's attention wasn't focussed on the TV but on the plain gold pocket watch in his hand. He glanced from the watch to the TV, pleased to see only a minute's difference between the two times. The watch had belonged to his grandfather, and it was a point of pride with the Lawrence men that it be kept in mint condition.

It was also tradition for it to be handed down to the eldest son, which left Micah in a quandary since his eldest son had no idea Micah was his father. Thirty-seven years ago, Micah had been in love with Ruby Delaney, or Ruby Jenkins as she'd been back then. His family had moved away, and he'd had no idea Ruby was pregnant when he left. When his parents divorced and he and his mother moved back to Lewiston a few years later, Ruby was married to Hutch Delaney and had a little boy. Ruby hadn't confessed to the truth until much later. To his knowledge Donovan never had been told.

Now Micah was toying with the idea of breaking his silence. The shooting of Rowland Hardisty and the need to find a matching blood donor had made Micah aware of the importance of knowing your medical history, but he, who wasn't afraid of much of anything, was terrified of telling Donovan he was his father. The Delaneys and the Hardistys and the Suttons had had their share of trouble the past few months, and Micah was loath to add to them. Still, he knew it should be done.

He rose and put the watch into the pocket of his slacks and turned off the television. It was time to get ready to go to work. He'd give himself a little more time to come to a final conclusion about Donovan. He would tell him. Sometime soon.

Rowland had always had a high tolerance for pain, and it had become something of a test to see how long he could go before giving in to the need for the medication, so the next time he was awakened by the pain, he refused to take anything for it. Even though there was considerable discomfort, he realized he was getting better.

He awakened and lay with his eyes closed, thinking about what the doctor had said to him about the importance of Cassidy giving blood. Again he asked himself why she'd done it.

A sound alerted him to the fact that someone was in the room. He shifted his legs and opened his eyes, turning his head toward the sound. Belle stood near the window and, hearing the rustle of the sheets, she turned. The expression in her eyes was both fearful and resolved. He'd seldom seen his granddaughter afraid of anything, but the determination was something he was very familiar with.

Belle, who had always seemed older than her age, was, like the woman she was named for, stubborn and outspoken. In the past few months she'd given advice to most of the grown-ups in her immediate family, telling them in no uncertain terms if she thought they were wrong and suggesting ways they could correct their sins. Rowland knew her well enough to know that something was on her mind, and—like it or not—he was about to find out what it was.

"Hi," he said.

She moved closer to the bed. "Hi. How do you feel?"

"Very sore, but better, I think."

"Good." She sat down in the chair sitting next to the bed. "You're very lucky, you know. Sheriff Lawrence said that if Carl Lawrey had been sober, you'd be a dead man."

"So they say. Where is everyone?"

"Everybody was here, but you were sleeping, so they went down to get something to eat. I wasn't hungry." Belle's fingers gripped the armrests, and she took a deep breath.

Here it comes.

"If it weren't for Cassidy, you might have died," she said. "You had to have some blood, and she was the only one whose blood was compatible, since Dad was in St. Louis."

"The doctor told me about that earlier," Rowland said.

"I know you don't like her, but I think the least you can do is tell her you appreciate what she did."

"I don't dislike her," Rowland said, aware—and not for the first time—that Belle was one sharp kid. "I just didn't want your father to marry Sophie, and I took it out not only on the two of them but Cassidy as well."

Which, when he gave it some serious thought was rather juvenile. Reed was a grown man, his marriage to Lara had been over for years. There was no reason he shouldn't marry whomever he thought would make him happy. There was always divorce if things didn't work out. Divorce. For the first time since being shot, Rowland wondered if Grace still planned to divorce him.

"You've been very mean to her," Belle said, bringing Rowland's thoughts back to the problem at hand.

"I realize that." He didn't recall such guilt being laid at his feet since he was a kid and stole some candy from the local grocery store.

"And what you did to Justine and Wes was mean, too. None of us understand why you go out of your way to hurt people."

The statement was one she'd no doubt heard from the adults in her life, which told Rowland he'd been discussed, and probably at length. He had no answer, since he didn't understand the compulsion, either. Maybe it was time to find out why he did the things he did.

"How did you find out about Justine and Wes?"

"I heard my mother and Donovan talking about it. Donovan said in a way you're responsible for Justine's wreck and that her baby was born early. He said if anything happens to the baby, it'll be on your conscience."

"How is the baby?" Rowland asked, trying to deflect the pang of guilt that shot through him at her words.

"He's doing okay," Belle said, the fire going out of her voice at mention of the baby. "Justine named him William Brady Grayson."

"Grayson?"

Belle nodded, her voice warming now that they were discussing the baby. "She didn't want to use Grayson, since she and Wes aren't married, but Uncle Wes said Will was a Grayson and he was going to wear the Grayson name. You know how he can be when he makes up his mind."

The latter statement sounded just like something Lara would say about her brother. Rowland heard a noise outside the door and turned as Cassidy poked her head in. When her eyes met his, she looked as if she would have liked to turn and run; instead, she resolutely pushed open the door and stepped through.

"Hello, Cassidy," he said.

"Hi."

Rowland turned to Belle. "Do you mind giving me and Cassidy a few moments?"

Belle and Cassidy exchanged wary looks, but Belle nodded and headed for the door.

Rowland pushed the bedside button to raise his upper part of the bed, wincing at the painfulness of the new position. Cassidy stared at a point near his head, but refused to look at him.

"Cassidy."

Her gaze darted to his.

"Belle tells me I've been mean to you and your mother." Cassidy didn't say anything, so Rowland continued. "She's right. I have been mean. And manipulative. I've heard whispers around the hospital through the years, people saying I have a God complex. I ignored the whispers, but since the other night I've begun to think they're right. Maybe I've carried the control I have in the operating room into my personal life…into the lives of my family. Maybe I like having things my way a little too much."

"Maybe you do," Cassidy said, raising her chin and fixing him with a steady look that reminded him of Belle.

"Admission is the first step to recovery, isn't it?"

"So they say."

"Well, I recognize that I've abused my knowledge and my power in certain situations, and I apologize for that. I'll try to do better."

"You need to apologize to a lot of people."

"I will." They stared at each other for several seconds, and Rowland realized that Cassidy was a very pretty girl. "Why did you do it?" he asked, finally.

Cassidy didn't ask what. She knew. "Because whether either one of us likes it or not, you're my grandfather. My mother taught me to respect my elders and to try to help people when I can."

So it was duty that prompted her. Rather than feel slighted, Rowland knew he should be grateful for whatever it was that caused her to make the offer. "Duty can be a drag, can't it?"

"Sometimes," she agreed. "But giving you a pint of blood wasn't a drag. You aren't really a part of my life, Mr. Hardisty, and you've done a lot of damage to our family, but regardless of that, I don't wish you any

harm. I don't hate you. I just think it's sad for you,
because your selfishness had turned my dad and almost
everyone in your life against you and made a lot of
people really unhappy. And I also think it's a shame
that you've missed out on so many good things.''

While Rowland mulled over that, Cassidy turned and
left the room, leaving him again with that strong sense
of chastisement. He didn't like what she'd said, but he
knew it was deserved. He was approaching his sixty-
third birthday, and it would be hard to change the attitudes and inclinations of a lifetime. Still, even though
they said it was impossible to teach an old dog new
tricks, he vowed to try. He would start with Grace.

All arguments had failed. She was going to Donovan's, and Wes was going to stay with her. Justine
wasn't sure she'd ever seen anyone as stubborn as Wes
Grayson, once he'd made up his mind about something.
Unfortunately for her, that current something was that
he was going to take care of her until she was able to
take care of herself.

At her request all the flowers that had been sent to
her from fans across the country were put in the rooms
of patients who were less fortunate than she. Wes
loaded her gifts into his car and wheeled her out of the
hospital amid a chorus of well-wishes. And here she
was, tucked into his car, her things stowed in the trunk,
on her way to Donovan's.

She had to give it to Wes, he'd been the epitome of
thoughtfulness the past couple of days. Telling him she
didn't want or need him there was like butting heads
with a billy goat. He'd stayed and literally hovered over
her. Almost every time she awakened, he was there demanding to know what she wanted, needed, giving her

an update on the baby. If things had been different, she might have appreciated his solicitousness, but she hadn't forgotten the look in his eyes as he'd demanded to know about her and his father.

She didn't blame him for feeling betrayed; betrayal was an emotion she'd been on close terms with for many years. The truth was that this newest wrinkle was one of those insurmountable obstacles life had a way of throwing in your path. By telling Wes about her and his father, Rowland had effectively ruined any hope of their having a future together. She knew Wes's behavior since the accident was based on the guilt he must be feeling for his liability for the accident.

"We're here."

Justine didn't answer. Her newest way of dealing with Wes was to ignore him as much as possible. Thank goodness they were home. She was still in a fair amount of pain—nothing that couldn't be managed with the occasional tablet—and far from feeling like her old self, but she grew stronger every day, and she was doing everything the doctors told her so that she could go and see the baby—Will—as soon as possible. She ached to hold him, ached to get him home so that the two of them could be a family. A family without a father, she reminded herself.

As they turned right, taking the leg of the Y that led to the house instead of the greenhouses, Donovan, who was on a golf cart, saw them and headed toward the house.

Wes pulled the car in front of the house, got out and came around to help her out. She turned, swinging her legs to the side and lowering them to the ground. Wes took her elbow, giving her some support as she eased from the car.

"Hi, Juss," Donovan said, leaning forward and dropping a kiss to her cheek.

"Hi, yourself," she said, flashing him a weary smile. Donovan turned to Wes. "Need any help?"

"You can help unload the car while I get her inside."

"Sure." Donovan went to the driver's side and popped open the trunk. "By the way, the door is unlocked. Sophie came over this morning to put fresh sheets on the bed in the master bedroom because the bathroom is closer. And she left lunch in the refrigerator."

"Great," Justine said, leaning on Wes as they started up the steps.

Donovan, loaded down with Justine's paraphernalia, reached the door before they did and pushed it open. The house was immaculate and smelled like something clean and fresh. Justine noticed that Sophie had scattered the bouquets she'd kept at strategic spots throughout the house. Wes helped Justine to the master bedroom, where he tucked her into the antique bed. An arrangement of daisies, statice and lilies sat on the dresser across the room where Justine could enjoy it.

"Need anything?" he asked, brushing back a strand of hair from her cheek.

Justine steeled herself against the magic of his touch and closed her eyes to block out the tenderness in his. "No. I'm going to try to sleep for a while."

Wes pulled the sheet and a light blanket up over her. "I'll be close if you need me."

She heard the door close behind him, and two tears squeezed their way from beneath her tightly shut eyes and trickled into the hair of her temples. She heard the low drone of the two men talking as she drifted into a sleep filled with dreams where she was grabbing for something just out of reach.

The next couple of days were spent resting and trying to build up her strength. Wes was with her most of the time, but he drove to Little Rock every afternoon to check on the baby in person. While he was gone, Donovan let her use one of his walkie-talkies in case she needed to reach him for anything.

In two days she was able to walk to the greenhouses and back, even though she wouldn't get any blue ribbons for speed. By the weekend Tom gave his okay, and she finally felt she was able to make the trip to Little Rock to see the baby, who—so far—hadn't had any serious problems. The fact that he was doing so well made her own predicament worthwhile. According to Sophie, Justine had already fallen into what Lara called the "mother mode."

A couple of days later, wearing a pretty, loose-fitting dress in a Hawaiian print, Justine and Wes set out for the hospital and her first visit with her son. She was too excited to think of any discomfort or weariness she might feel. When they reached the nursery, they were told they were expected. A nurse handed them disposable scrubs and instructed them to put them on over their clothes. Then they were led to a small room, where Will's incubator had been moved, so that they could spend some time with him.

When Justine saw the patches over his eyes and all the tubes and machines, she promptly burst into tears. Wes put his arm around her and held her close, rubbing his hands up and down her back. "I should have warned you. I know it looks pretty scary, but it isn't as bad as it seems."

As he explained what all the paraphernalia was for, Justine's tears and her fear subsided somewhat. Wes encouraged her to insert her hands into the ports on the side of the incubator, so she could touch him. "He's so tiny. What if I hurt him?"

"You won't."

Justine did as he instructed, and touched Will's arm. It was incredibly soft. With tears streaming down her cheeks, she ran her palm over his leg and counted his toes, even though it was clear to see they were all there.

"Talk to him," Wes said. "They say it's good for him to hear your voice. And he'll know yours."

"I used to sing to him."

"Then sing."

She did. She didn't know if Will recognized her voice, but there was something about doing it that brought Justine a measure of comfort. After thirty minutes the sheer emotional impact of the visit had taken its toll, and Wes said it was time to go.

They hardly spoke on the way back to Lewiston. Justine was too busy reliving her visit with her son and grieving over the fact that Rowland had ruined any chance she, the baby and Wes had of being a real family.

"I know what happened."

The sound of Wes's voice broke the stillness and intruded on Justine's misery. She noticed they were at the Lewiston city limits.

"What happened when?" she asked, but her heart had started to beat faster.

"With you and my dad." Before she could comment, he said, "Sophie showed me the diary."

Justine couldn't think of anything to say. All she could do was stare at him in disbelief.

"After the accident I called Sophie and asked her if I could talk to her. She agreed. I went over and told her about what happened with Rowland. She said there was something I should see, and she called Molly and had her bring the diary over."

Feeling the prickling of tears, Justine turned away and looked out the passenger side window.

"I know about my dad being Molly's dad, too," he said. "Lara agrees that she deserves her third of what Dad left us."

Justine closed her eyes and gave a sigh of thankfulness. The generosity was what she'd expected, but somehow, after all they'd been through, it was nice to know her trust in Wes and Lara was deserved.

Wes flipped on his turn signal and pulled into the city park.

"What are you doing?"

"Pulling over so we can talk about this face-to-face."

"We've tried talking about it, and you didn't want to hear what I had to say."

"I was hurt."

She sucked in a sharp breath of surprise.

"But that's no excuse. Look at me, Justine."

Despite her pounding heart, she did as he asked.

"What Rowland said caught me completely off guard. It's nothing I would have suspected if I'd had a thousand guesses. I was hurt and angry, and my ego was bruised a little. I felt as if you'd betrayed me."

Justine felt tears filling her eyes and pressed her lips together to keep them from trembling.

"You tried to explain, and I wouldn't listen. I feel as if your accident was my fault."

"Is that why you've been so attentive?" she asked

in a trembling voice. "To try to salve your guilty conscience?"

"No," he said, his voice husky with emotion. "Though I do feel responsible. I've spent so much time with you since the accident, because almost losing you made me realize that nothing in the past mattered."

"The past does matter," she said. "You'll never forget what I did."

"Neither will you. But I know now why it happened. I know it wasn't your doing. And I know that I don't want to spend the rest of my life without you in it."

Justine stared at him, her eyes searching his, seeing nothing but sincerity.

"As far as I'm concerned, Gene Malone should be taken out and horsewhipped. Sophie and I have talked a lot the past few days, and she's made me understand how you must have felt, the kind of pressure you were under. That's one reason I want Molly to have the money she deserves. I don't want her to ever be put in a position where she has to choose the wrong thing for all the right reasons."

Silent tears slipped down Justine's cheeks. "Thank you for that."

He nodded and reached out to trail a finger along the sweet-curving line of her cheek. "Marry me, Justine, and let's make a home for our son."

A few days ago his offer had been enough. She shook her head. "I can't, Wes. Not now."

"Why?"

"Because the accident and the baby's birth made me aware just how fragile and precious life is. I'm not willing to settle for a marriage without love, even though there are no guarantees that that love will last."

"I do love you."

She laughed, and more tears slipped down her cheeks. "What you feel for me isn't love, and you know it."

"Yes, I do want you," he said, exasperation lacing his voice. "God knows I've never wanted another woman the way I want you, but that isn't all there is to it. I never really got over you, Justine. I always wondered why you left, and I always wondered if you ever thought about me the way I thought about you. That's why I looked you up in Chicago. Because I hadn't forgotten you and I was curious to see if what I felt was still there. It's taken me a long time to realize my feelings for what they are, so don't you dare presume to tell me what I feel isn't the real thing."

When she didn't answer, he started the car.

"Where are we going?"

"To my place. I have something to show you."

Neither spoke as they made the trip to the cabin. Wes helped her out of the car and into the house, leading her to the room where he did his painting and putting her in a chair in the middle of the room. Then he started pulling out paintings. There was one of her onstage, wearing the outfit she'd worn the night she'd performed in Chicago. There was a Mardi Gras ball painting—a ballroom she recognized as the ballroom from Nottoway Plantation—the room filled with people. On closer examination, she recognized that every female face, though covered with some sort of mask, was hers. There was a picture of her on the dock, though she'd never been there until the night of the accident. One of her lying on a pile of pillows in the johnboat. There were dozens of paintings of her that he'd done since their encounter in Chicago, and he'd done them all from memory.

Clearly she'd been on his mind. The sheer number of the paintings and the obvious care and passion that had driven him was overwhelming. And more convincing than anything he could ever have said to her. A picture was indeed worth a thousand words.

As she looked up at him, fighting back the tears again, he dropped to his knees in front of her and took the hand that wasn't hindered by the cast into both of his. "As far as I'm concerned, our past began in Chicago."

"Wes…"

"Shh," he said, and pressed a kiss to the palm of her hand. When he raised his head to look at her, there were tears in his eyes. "Yes, I feel guilt because my anger drove you away, but that isn't the reason I want to marry you. And I don't want to marry you to give the baby my name. I've already done that. I want to marry you because I've been alone too long. I've been lonely too long."

Justine curled her fingers around his. Wes leaned forward and licked away the tear that had gathered in the corner of her mouth, then he kissed her, a whisper-soft kiss that felt like the promise of a thousand tomorrows.

"Marry me, Justine," he whispered against her mouth. "Marry me, and I'll spend a lifetime trying to make you happy."

Justine nodded and turned into his kiss, this one filled with enough heat to seal their love and their promises for a lifetime.

Epilogue

Seven months later

Justine sat in a rocking chair on the patio behind her new house, Will cradled in her arms, giving him a bottle. The soft April breeze blew his dark hair and fluttered the bright fabric Justine had wrapped around her swimsuit when she'd finished tanning. She smiled down at the baby, even though his eyes were closed. At seven months, he was perfectly healthy, if a little small for his age. He was perfect, and her husband, if not so perfect, was close enough. Perfect would be boring, and life with Wes was anything but that. While living with another artistic person was sometimes hard, there were also times when something came up that the other person understood without question—like when the creative muse flew in from Tahiti, or wherever it went when

it wasn't in residence on Crescent Lake and the lyrics
had to be written or the painting finished. Whatever life
with Wes was, she wouldn't have changed it for anything.

In the months since Will's birth a lot of other changes
had taken place. Lara was pregnant—with a boy—and
the baby was due in June. She planned on working
through the end of the school year and taking off at
least a year from her job of high school principal. Belle
was ecstatic over the prospect of having a new baby
brother.

Grace Hardisty had gone through with her divorce,
just as Lara predicted, and was currently seeing a widower and former lawyer from Texarkana. Rowland was
taking it as well as a man used to having his own way
could. He had made some drastic changes in his life
and his attitudes, even though some of them had come
too late. His relationship with Reed, Sophie and Cassidy
was improving, though they were far from being close.

Sophie and Reed were still deliriously happy, and
Sophie's family counseling clinic was a success. Molly
was engaged and her relationship with Justine was
growing stronger by the day.

Cassidy was thrilled that Jett Robbins would soon be
coming home for the summer, though Sophie worried
about Cass's feelings for the older boy. She didn't want
her and Reed's history repeating itself with her daughter
and Jett. Justine told her not to worry—Cassidy had a
good head on her shoulders.

Wes had finished the paintings for his show with the
Culligan Gallery, and despite her absence from the
Nashville scene, another song from Justine's CD had
climbed to number three on the country charts. She

leaned her head back and looked up at the lacy canopy of leaves above her. Life was good, very good.

"Madonna and child."

The sound of Wes's voice brought a smile to her lips, but she didn't open her eyes. In a moment she felt his mouth against her throat. "Mmm," she murmured in pleasure.

"Exactly," Wes said, easing his hands under the baby and lifting him into his own arms. He bounced Will a few times and then lowered him gently into the playpen Justine had placed beneath the shade of the giant oak tree that protected the deck and propped his bottle with a stuffed toy. Then he pulled Justine to her feet and led her to the quilt where she'd suntanned earlier.

He leaned forward and kissed her, his hands working the knot of the gauzy fabric tied around her hips. Justine's hands found the buckle of his belt. As she slipped it from the loops, he wrapped his fingers around the straps of her swimsuit and tugged them down her arms, baring her breasts to the heat of his gaze and the gentleness of his touch.

He kissed her, and his hands began their familiar magic.

"Mmm," she moaned again, pressing against him.

He laughed against her lips. "Did anyone ever tell you that you have a very limited vocabulary, Mrs. Grayson?"

"I can't think when you touch me," she whispered.

Then, somehow, there were no clothes to hamper them. Wes's weight was a sweet burden, his touch the fuel to the flame his kisses ignited. Would she ever get used to the heady breathlessness he made her feel?

Would she ever tire of the feel of his hands on her, of his body and lips against hers?

Doubtful.

"I have only one regret," he breathed into her ear several kisses later.

"What's that?" she asked, her nails digging into his back as she gasped for air.

"I didn't get to paint you pregnant."

"This time you can," she whispered against his lips. "This time."

* * * * *

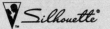

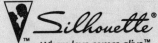

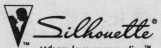

If you enjoyed what you just read,
then we've got an offer you can't resist!

Take 2 bestselling
love stories FREE!
Plus get a FREE surprise gift!